blunts tails volume 2

A DADDY P.I. SHORT STORY COLLECTION

E J FROST

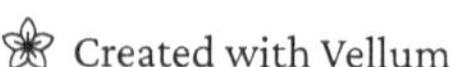 Created with Vellum

For my beloved patrons, who kept encouraging me in this madness and helped shape each story.
For my amazing, wonderful, giving, and stunningly sharp-eyed alpha readers, Bianca Williams and Michelle Gong. I very literally could not do this without you now.

a notorious tail — part 1

MASTER IAN AND BRIAR ROSE - BRENNA

"BREN, YOUR TWO O'CLOCK IS HERE."

I lift my head hazily from my desk as the intercom buzzes and Taco announces my client.

The desk rocks under me from the force of Mac's thrusts. I put my head back down. My client's early and I know better than to interrupt my Sir mid-fuck. He'll have timed everything so I'm ready for my appointment.

I trust my Sir.

Mac plants his hand on the desk beside my head as his pace increases. I ride the waves of sensation. He's already given me two orgasms. I'm slipping and sliding through the afterglow while he finishes.

He groans, deep and low, and slides his other hand up my back, pushing me flat onto the desk. I shiver with the pressure on my breasts and tip my ass up further. Mac pounds into me, hard and bruising as he chases his release. With another guttural groan, he releases his heat into me.

I sigh with satisfaction. If there's a better feeling than my Sir coming in me, I haven't felt it yet.

He leans over me, still holding me down, making me feel his mastery. I wallow in contentment. Mac kisses my bare shoulder, his lips a soft contrast to the nip of his teeth. "Who shows up thirty minutes early for a tattoo?"

"Virgin," I tell him. Only tattoo virgins show up this early. Particularly when I've already done the design based on what he sent me by email and he's approved it, so there's nothing we need to get out of the way before I fire up my gun. "Thank you for my orgasms and for coming in me, Sir."

He bites down, hard enough to leave the impression of his teeth. Hard enough to send a spark of heat through me. "You're welcome, girl. Stay still while I clean you up."

I tuck my arm under my head and rest my cheek on my wrist, relaxing while my Sir takes care of me. He cleans off the sweat of our exertions with baby wipes—no better way to get sweaty in my opinion—and tidies up my pussy and ass, since he's made thorough use of both. He even lifts my bare feet from the floor and wipes between my toes, which makes me giggle and grin like an idiot.

He returns my grin before tapping my ass to let me know he's done. I straighten and pull on my clothes from where he draped them over my desk chair after I gave him the strip-tease he demanded before his lunch-time fuck.

Mac parks his naked ass in my chair and watches me dress. His face is soft, no lines of tension on his brow or around his mouth. His eyes are a clear, August-sky blue. The defined muscles of his chest and abs are relaxed, just dimples under his skin.

My Sir's had a lot to worry about lately, but today, he's happy. With his daughter living in my old apartment upstairs, he's within a hundred feet of his family. Naomi seems to be settling into a good routine. She's taken the semester off from college, but she's still meeting with her tutors twice a week and easing her way back into studying. She's helping Mac at his new daycare three mornings a week and has a real gift for creating fun math puzzles for the five preschoolers.

She even went on a date last night.

Logan, Emily, and I had to physically restrain Mac from chaperoning the date. Since it was with Master Martin from Blunts, I understood Mac's anxiety. But I also know Master Martin will give Naomi the gentlest introduction to kink of any human being on the planet.

I don't want to tell Mac why I know that because then he'll ask if I've scened with Martin. I don't lie to my Sir, but Mac really would not be happy if he knew I've had sex dozens of time with the man who gave Naomi her first taste of kink last night.

Fortunately, he hasn't asked, so I haven't had to rob his August-sky eyes of their happy light.

"Toss me my boxers, girl."

I scoop them up off the floor, but instead of throwing them to Mac, I kneel at his feet.

His grin spreads wide as he lifts one foot and then the other. I slide the boxers up to his thighs and let him pull them up the rest of the way. I place a kiss on each of his knees, now adorned in colorful ink from the leg pieces I've designed for him, before I rise.

"Nicely done, girl. What're you angling for?"

I button up my shirt before putting my hands behind my back and adopting an air of innocence that I've learned from Emily. "Me, Sir?"

He snorts, not at all fooled. "You, girl."

"Master Logan *might* have mentioned that *if* the membership vote goes your way, you'll be asked to do several scenes to prove your mastery. Since Mistress Dana, Master Karl, and Master Franco make up the membership sub-committee and they're all big fans of whipping, they'd be impressed by your skill with a signal whip. I was just thinking we could practice tonight, if you wanted to, Sir."

"I like your line of thinking. Since Taco's here, I'll head out, make us an early dinner, and we'll watch a game to let our food digest before a scene at nine. What's your earliest appointment tomorrow?"

"I'm not on until noon."

"Perfect. You'll be able to walk by then."

I wriggle in excitement. "Yes, Sir."

Mac chuckles as he hauls himself lazily out of his chair and pulls on his shirt. "I love your enthusiasm, girl. Give me a kiss before you get back to work."

I go up on my toes and give him a very prim, chaste peck.

With a growl, Mac grabs me, crushes me to him, and stamps my mouth with his. All the hunger, possessiveness, and dominance that my Sir is growing unashamed to show flows through me with the seeking, searching movement of his lips and tongue. I melt and wriggle up tightly against him and let him own me.

He looks into my eyes as he slowly releases me. "Getting to be that time, girl."

"What time is that, Sir? Kinda early for dinner."

Or round three since I'm a little sore, but I'd *never* tell Mac that. Red flag. Bull.

"Time for you to share my name and wear another of my rings."

Melt. Shiver. The tail I don't have wags.

"Ready whenever you are, Sir."

"Mmm. I don't want to upstage the wedding of the century, but it's getting to be time and past time, girl. Be ready, 'cause some day soon I'm going to put you on the back of my bike, ride you off to a quiet little church somewhere, and make an honest woman of you."

I laugh at his reference to Emily and Logan's upcoming wedding, which truly is taking on A-list celebrity proportions, despite Emily's best attempts to keep it intimate. Then I straighten my face and look right back into his eyes.

"Any time. Anywhere, Sir."

He chucks me under the chin before he lets me go.

Walking on clouds rather than my Docs, I drift out of my office and into the front of the shop.

Where Superman is waiting for me.

I do a double-take.

"Uh."

He grins.

Superman just grinned at me.

I slump onto the arm of one of the reception couches. I was giddy after that go-round with Mac, but now I'm honestly faint. Why is Superman in my shop? And am I really going to give Superman a tattoo?

No, I'm not. I'm going to have to get Taco to sub in for me. There's no way I can keep my hands off Superman and it's a toss-up who would kill me first: Mac or the State of New York for molesting a national treasure. Does New York still have the death penalty? If not, they'd definitely make an exception if Superman accused me of groping him while I was giving him a tattoo.

"I, uh—" I try weakly.

He chuckles. "My name's Ian. I'm a lookalike and stunt double."

"Uh." My brains have left the building. "Oh."

"He loves your tattoo design, by the way. I sent it to his publicist. He's not interested in getting a tattoo, but his publicist said they'd keep your details on file in case he wants one in the future."

"Bu-but, if you get a tattoo he doesn't have—"

Ian flashes me that multi-million-dollar smile. He even has the same dimples. I really might faint.

"I can cover it with body paint. I have to do that for a couple of scars anyway if I'm going to take off my shirt. Don't worry about it."

"Uh. Okay."

"Are you alright?"

He looks exactly like the Man of Steel asking Lois Lane that. Exactly. I know, because Emily and I have watched the movie about a hundred times. She has her thing for X-Men and yeah, I would not kick Gambit out of bed, but I'm a DC girl all the way. Give me fucking Superman.

"Uh."

There's a chorus of chuckles from behind me.

Fuckers.

I turn and glare at the trio clustered around the reception desk who are sniggering at my expense. It does not make me happy to see that my Sir has joined Taco and Nicky in the peanut gallery.

"Okay," I say, pulling my act together. "Any changes to the design I emailed you?"

"No," Superman says, smiling that ovary-shredding smile again. "It's perfect."

Like his teeth. "Okay, follow me."

He pushes up off the couch with just the strength of his rippling thighs. Damn. I avert my eyes and scuttle over to the reception desk to print off the design. Taco hands it to me with a shit-eating grin; he'll be lucky if I don't make it permanent.

I stick my fingers in Taco's dimples and make a buzzing sound that sobers him up quickly. I've threatened to give him "a Joker" more than once.

I flap the thermofax at the men to disperse their unholy coven. And the Blunts Doms say subs are bad.

An hour later, Ian—who I've managed to retrain my brain into thinking of as Ian and not Superman—has a field of poppies blooming across his left pec in memory of his grandmother. He winced a couple of times, but otherwise bore the pain of his first tattoo like a champ.

I spin on my stool while I wait for him to put his shirt and sweater back on. He perches on the edge of the tattoo table and looks at me with those blue-blue eyes.

"So, I have to ask," he says.

"About the aftercare? I have a card for you that explains everything."

He tips his head to the side. "Aftercare. Hm. I couldn't help but notice that you wear a collar. Any chance it means what I hope it means?"

Kinky Superman. I'm going to die.

"What do you hope it means?" I ask, somehow without stuttering.

"I hope it means you're a submissive. And since you're not wearing a wedding ring, I really hope it means you'd be open to going for a coffee with me."

"It does mean what you think it means, but the lack of ring doesn't. I take my rings off when I'm working. I'm engaged. But." I hold up a finger. "If you're open to the lifestyle and looking for people to connect with, I know a bunch of collar-wearing people who would love to meet you."

An idea blooms. A wonderful, terrible idea.

"In fact, is there *any* chance you're free tomorrow night?"

"I am." The dimples appear again.

I grab a notepad and a pen and write down the Blunts nightclub address and the codeword that will get Ian into the VIP upper level. "This is a nightclub where I dance two nights a week. Full of collar-wearing people. Want to have some fun with them?"

"Fun that involves you calling me by The Famous Guy's name?" Ian asks.

I tap the tip of my nose with my finger.

"I'm good with it as long as we tell everyone the truth before the end of the night. I can't do anything that might tarnish his public image."

"No problem. There's tons of security at the club. No paparazzi. No reporters. No phones or cameras in that part of the club. My collar-wearing friends love a joke, so they'll take it well. And if you like the club, you'll be welcome back to meet more collar-wearing people."

"Can't argue with that."

"My shift starts at nine, but I usually get there an hour in advance to hang out and see people. If you're there before nine, I'll introduce you."

"As The Famous Guy. To collar-wearing people."

I laugh. With his slightly sarcastic sense of humor, he'll fit right in at Blunts.

He offers me his hand and I shake, then give him the tattoo after-care card.

[To be continued . . .]

a notorious tail — part 2

MASTER IAN AND BRIAR ROSE - IAN

I'D BE LYING if I said I wasn't slightly disappointed that the woman who got me to this quiet street in Lenox Hill on a Thursday night is wearing not just another man's collar but also another man's ring.

And I try not to lie to myself.

I saw the glances Brenna exchanged with the older guy at the desk. I figure he's her Dom. There's something about the heat and knowingness of those looks that gives it away. I exchanged them with Amber for years; I miss being both the giver and receiver.

But Amber moved on and it's time I did, too. It's a shame that the first woman who made my submissive radar ping *and* my blood stir is taken. I liked Brenna before I asked her out for coffee; her kindness as she let me down only made me like her more. But if she's engaged, then she's off-limits. The idea of breaking up a couple makes my skin crawl. I'll never be "the other guy."

Before I meet Brenna at the address she's given me, I try to research it. Is it an underground munch? A rave for kinksters?

All I can find is a well-reviewed Italian restaurant at one end of the building and a nightclub that's been going for nearly a century in the basement. The space in between the restaurant and nightclub is indicated as a "private club and spa" in everything I can find. I like a facial as much as the next man—more when I'm giving than when I'm receiving, although I've done both—but surely the whole building can't be a spa? It's almost an entire city block. In the middle of Manhattan. That's a lot of lotion and hot rocks.

There's no sign. No floodlights. No red carpet when I arrive at the address. A short line of people wait on the sidewalk. But for the fish-nets and leather pants in the crowd, they could be waiting for a bus. A bouncer even wider than I am, and I work out every day to keep up with The Famous Guy's physique, polices the line. He waves me forward when I approach. When I show him the code word Brenna's given me, he opens the velvet rope, clips a white bracelet to my wrist, and gestures to the inner door.

"Stop at the cloak room on the left past the doors and show them your bracelet. They'll give you instructions."

I nod my thanks and ignore the faint whispers of "Superman" and "Witcher" that follow me through the door and down the stairs.

Because Brenna said we were going to have fun with her friends tonight, I've styled and dressed to look like The Famous Guy. I got the tattoo, which is a work of art I'll be proud to wear all my life, right after I'd done an appearance so I still had the temporary color in my hair and the contacts in when Brenna met me. When I'm not in role, I let my natural brown and green show and dress for comfort rather than flare. People still mistake me for The Famous Guy on first glance, but on a second glance, they give me a sheepish smile and edge away without asking for a picture and autograph.

The smiling blonde who greets me from behind the desk in the small coat room doesn't give me a second glance. Either she's so used to seeing celebrities that The Famous Guy doesn't rate, or she's just very well trained. I notice a thin brown leather collar tucked just inside the neckline of the little black dress she's wearing. It's a different color than Brenna's, but otherwise identical.

Collar-wearing friends, indeed.

The blonde details the club's layout for me: the long dance floor, the illuminated areas that are to be kept clear, and the mezzanine level that Brenna's code word gives me access to. The blonde explains that the mezzanine is color coded. Red areas are for dancing, drinking, and socializing, but no scenes. Green areas are scene areas.

My blood kicks up another notch at the idea of designated scene areas.

The blonde shows me her collar and says that anyone wearing a similar leather collar and a pink wristlet on the mezzanine level is a house submissive, employed by the club. They're available for non-sexual scenes after verbal negotiation. Full nudity or penetration is prohibited on the mezzanine.

She says all of this with a small smile but an otherwise straight face. Not exactly bored, but this is all business as usual for her.

Not for me. My blood's pounding in my ears and I feel like a kid on Christmas morning.

She shows me the alert button on my wristlet that will summon security, takes my phone, writes a locker number on my wristlet, and wishes me a good night.

I thank her warmly. If I trot away through the club to the elevator up to the mezzanine level like my Armani-suited tail is on fire, no one comments or stops me. So maybe it's not an unusual reaction.

I'm grinning ear to ear when the elevator doors open and the mezzanine level spreads to either side of me. It's a twenty-foot-wide platform wrapping around three sides of the long space. The mezzanine is at the same height as three cages which hang over the dance floor. They're currently empty, but the DJ is already in his booth, warming up with techno tracks that will have the dance floor heaving in no time once the doors open.

I haven't paid much attention to the club's décor in my excitement, but up here, in better lighting, it's impossible to miss. 1920s Art Deco. Gold glints everywhere. A long, frosted-glass bar dominates the end of the mezzanine furthest from the outer door. I wouldn't be surprised to find that the bar only serves Sidecars and Gin Rickeys. Tables with fringed lamps built into them, surrounded by clusters of gracefully curved, wrought iron chairs, dot expanses of rich red carpeting. Every twenty feet, the red carpet is broken by an emerald-green square. The squares are mostly empty, but there's a metal St. Andrew's cross erected in one and spanking benches in two others.

Blood's pounding so loudly in my ears, I couldn't tell you what the DJ's playing.

Movement at one of the tables catches my eye. Brenna, with her eye-catching blue dreadlocks, half-rises and waves at me.

My mouth drops open. What is she wearing?

Not just Brenna, I realize as I move toward them at a speed much too fast to be casual. Most of the women at her table and the others nearby are wearing variations of the same outfit: black patent heels that make their legs look miles long, flashes of skin peeking through fishnet stockings, suspenders that make my fingers itch to unclip them, tiny satin panties, and a lace-up corset that creates plumper, more perfect cleavage than any Beverly Hills surgeon.

I have died and gone straight to subbie heaven.

There are men, too. The women are so gorgeous I almost overlook them, but a slender, black-haired man with bone structure so delicate he looks carved from marble is impossible not to see. He stands and holds a chair for me when I approach the table.

"Guest of honor," he says with a wry tilt to his lips.

"Everyone, this is—" Brenna begins.

She's interrupted by a strawberry blonde at a neighboring table who stands and sways in my direction. "My laws, it's such an honor to have you here."

She extends a manicured hand to me. Her pink French tips narrow to scary points, but a Dom knows no fear. I take her hand and kiss her knuckles. Putting on a faint British accent, I say, "Pleased to meet you."

She flutters fake lashes that brush her eyebrows. "Sorry, I'm havin' such a fan-girl moment."

I give her a patented Famous Guy smile that I've practiced a thousand times in the mirror.

She sits in the chair that the black-haired man held out for me and turns cornflower blue eyes up to me, rolling them in an unmistakable manner.

I don't need to be a Dom to know that look. Any man who's had a woman on her knees knows it. And my blood leaps predictably.

But my Dom-dar also pings. A man could drown in those wide blue eyes and that's exactly what she's angling for. She doesn't want a Dom. She wants someone to consume.

The black-haired man snags an empty chair from a nearby table and offers it to me. "Thank you," I tell him.

He nods. "I'm Cappa. Welcome."

I hold out my hand. His palm is cold against mine and I wonder if it's the air-conditioning, which is blasting for it being November, but I guess they're cooling down against the coming body heat, or if he's unwell.

As soon as I sit, the strawberry blonde scoots her chair a few inches closer. Close enough for me to feel the heat of her thigh against mine. Predatorial body heat.

"I didn't introduce myself," she says breathily. "I'm Briar Rose."

"Nice to meet you, Briar Rose."

"Oh, please, call me Briar. Can I get you anything? There's no alcohol on this level but I could get you a seltzer?"

"A seltzer would be nice, thank you."

I reach into my breast pocket for my wallet but she taps the back of my hand.

"No charge for VIPs." She flutters the lashes at me again before she jumps out of her seat, incredibly balanced on her stilettos, and prances off to the bar.

I'm weak enough to watch her go. And appreciate the view. And consider that it would improve with a tail plug.

I clear my throat and look back at the circle of people I haven't yet met because Briar Rose has successfully monopolized my attention.

My eyes land first on Brenna's wry grin. "So, you've met Briar," she says.

I chuckle. "She's quite a fan. I notice she's wearing a collar." I glance back and check her wrist. "And a pink band. I take it she's available for scenes?"

Brenna sucks her cheeks in. "Oh, yeah. One hundred and fifty percent available."

No love lost there, I gather.

"And are we telling her or not telling her first?"

Brenna's grin grows a sharp edge. "Not would be my preference. Let her enjoy her 'moment in the sun'." She frames the words with long, inked fingers.

I lift my eyebrows at her. "This isn't malicious, right?"

Beside me, Cappa coughs.

I glance around the table at a lot of guilty faces. One woman, who could be Cappa's twin with her cap of dark, silky hair and eyes a brighter blue than even The Famous Guy's, looks away, her face flushing nearly purple.

I shake my head at them. "I won't be part of something malicious."

Brenna wrinkles her nose at me. "Spoilsport."

"You said your friends love a joke. This doesn't feel like a joke."

Brenna rolls her eyes to the ceiling. "Ooookay. Tell her when she gets back. Crush her dreams. Be that guy."

I will. I like a joke as much as the next person, and looking so much like The Famous Guy, this isn't the first time I've gotten involved in one. But I never want to hurt anyone with it and it feels like Briar Rose will be genuinely wounded when she finds out the truth.

The rest of the submissives around the table introduce themselves. The woman with the arresting blue eyes can barely hold my gaze as she says, "Charlotte. Please call me Char."

Whatever strange alchemy it is that draws man to woman, Dominant to submissive, draws me much more strongly to Char than to the woman who returns with a glass of fizzing water.

Before Briar Rose sits down, I stand and touch her elbow. "Could I have a word?"

She looks up at me with a star-struck smile I've seen too many times before. Definitely time to nip this in the bud.

When she nods, I lead her a few steps away from the table. "I didn't want this to go any further. I'm not who you think I am. My name's Ian."

Her pink-glossed mouth drops in a silent O. She blinks and then smiles brightly. "I understand. I'll call you Ian."

"You'll call me Ian because that's my name," I say firmly. "I'm a stand-in and stunt double. I'm not him."

She winks. "Of course not."

"Briar—"

"Yes, Ian. I understand. I do. I'll call you whatever you like. Would you mind if I called you sir? I was wondering, well, hoping really, that we could do a scene before I have to go upstairs? I'd never be so forward ordinarily. It's just that I'm scheduled to be on the desk upstairs at nine, so I don't have much time."

I blow out a frustrated breath. I've tried to ensure she's not deceived; she seems to be willfully misunderstanding. Maybe that's her kink?

"Sure," I say. "I'd be happy to."

That's not entirely true. I'd rather she acknowledged I'm not The Famous Guy before scening with me. And part of me would rather be scening with Char. But this isn't an opportunity to pass up. It's been over a year since Amber and I went our separate ways. I'm ready to be a Dom again, even if only for a short scene with a submissive I'm not sure of.

"If you want," Briar says, sliding her hands behind her in a pose

I'm sure she knows is catnip for a Dom and thrusts her already impressive breasts under my nose, "we could go up into one of the private rooms."

I shake my head firmly. Anything I do tonight will be out in the open. I'm not yet sure of this place or these people and while I'm dressed and styled like The Famous Guy, I'm not doing anything that could open either of us to ugly speculation.

"I'd rather use the St. Andrew's cross over there, if you don't mind," I say. "Would you hold some positions for me?"

She twists from side to side so her breasts bob. "I'd be honored, sir."

As we walk over to the cross, I ask her about her limits, triggers, and safe words. She's very clear and definitive in responding, which settles the faint churn in my gut. Despite her capacity for self-deception, Briar Rose seems professional about the mechanics of submission.

Which makes me wonder.

"Before we begin, I'd like to ask you a question, if I may." At her nod, I continue, "What is this place? Is it a lifestyle nightclub? Are you employed here? I'm just a little confused about your role."

She smiles sunnily. "I was confused at first, too. The nightclub is part of a gentlemen's club that's been going since the eighteen-somethings. Oldest gentlemen's club in New York, I'm told. It's members only upstairs, but the nightclub and the restaurant are open to people in the lifestyle a few nights a week."

"Ah, that makes sense. And you?"

"I'm a house submissive. We're employed by Blunts. Most of them—" She nods at the table we've left behind. "Work the nightclub. They dance and wait tables in the VIP sections. I'm just down here visiting, but usually I work upstairs in the members-only area."

That leaves me with a burning question. But some instinct keeps me from asking Briar Rose. It's a question for Brenna, or maybe Char.

"I see," I say instead. "I'd like to address you as 'submissive' during the scene. Is that okay with you?"

She nods. "Anything you like, sir."

"Good. Submissive, please stand with your back against the cross."

She moves gracefully into position. I walk around behind her. The cross is positioned facing the open floor below. There are a few people moving around on the dance floor, although it's clear the club isn't open yet. Other VIPs? Members? The thought of membership in an exclusive lifestyle club is so tantalizing it pulls my head out of the scene for a moment. Amber found a few swingers parties for us to go to, but mostly we played on our own, in the privacy of our apartment. That this huge place is entirely devoted to the activities that gave me so much satisfaction and fulfillment makes my head spin.

I pull it firmly back where it belongs. Whatever Briar Rose's personal shortcomings, she's my submissive for the space of the scene and she deserves my full attention.

"Close your eyes, submissive," I tell her. "Listen to my voice."

She shivers and wriggles until her shoulders and ass touch the cross. "Yes, sir."

"Lift your arms slowly. Reach up until you find the arms of the cross. There are handles. Grasp the handles comfortably."

She follows direction. She's clearly not familiar with this cross because she fumbles around for the handles and only finds them by bringing her hands back down near her head and patting her way up the arms until she reaches the handles. While she's finding the handles, I glance back over at Brenna's table. Brenna's tipped back in her chair, talking to a tall, bald man who is standing over her, but the rest of the submissives are watching me.

It's a little unnerving, being the object of so many stares. I'm used to it at public events, but not in this place, doing these things. I divert myself by taking off my suit jacket and rolling up the sleeves of my dress shirt.

When I look back up, some eyes have wandered away. The twin blue gazes of Char and Cappa are riveted on my forearms.

I smile to myself. A lot of submissives have a thing for strong forearms and big hands. I know I have the goods in those departments. I nod at them before focusing on Briar Rose.

"Arch your back, submissive. Show me you're proud of your body."

She shifts her heels backward a fraction, then stretches away from the cross, hanging from the cross' handles to create a perfect bow.

"Nicely done," I praise her. "Lift your right leg, knee bent, and show me how good your balance is."

She doesn't even wobble on the high heels as she lifts her leg. Her thigh muscle flexes. It's a thing of beauty, a woman's flesh constrained by the black webbing of fishnets.

"Beautiful. Perfect balance. Leg down. Open your eyes and lift your chin."

She does and I reach around her to stroke my forefinger down from the tip of her chin to the base of her throat, enjoying the smooth, warm skin.

"Chin up, always," I say to her, dropping my voice as low as it goes, a bass rumble. "Submission is one of the hardest, noblest things a person can do. Be proud of your submission."

She blinks rapidly and presses her lips together.

I check in. "Submissive, is everything okay?"

"Yes, sir. Someone else told me to be proud of my collar recently. I guess . . . I guess I could do better at that."

"I'm pleased I could give you something to think on. Last position. All the way up on your toes. Stretch as high as you can."

She rolls forward onto the balls of her feet and stretches her whole body. Some knot of tension in her back pops and she lets out a soft sigh.

That sigh shoots right through me. It makes my whole body smile. This scene hasn't been a turn on the way scenes with Amber were. I don't have that spark with Briar Rose and I doubt getting to know her better will change that. But whatever it is that makes me a Dom derives deep satisfaction out of submission in any flavor. Just these few minutes controlling this woman fill an empty space in my soul.

"Release the cross, turn, and curtsy to me. I'll bow to you and that ends our scene, submissive."

As she does, I step out from behind the cross so we're facing each other. A soft, sweet, genuine smile lights her face. I return it as I bow deeply to her.

"Thank you for the scene, Briar."

"Thank you, Ian. May I kiss your cheek?"

I nod and angle my face for the brush of her lips. She thanks me again and then runs off toward the elevator, waving at the other collared-people as she goes.

I return to Brenna's table. I haven't had my eyes on my drink the whole time I've been scening with Briar Rose, so I take it back to the bar and get a fresh one. As I'm waiting, Char edges up beside me. I turn off the practiced charm and give her a real smile.

"I was hoping we'd have a chance to talk," I say to her.

"Oh? Would you like to scene?"

Not tonight. My well is full for now and I already know that what I want to do with this woman I do not want to do out in public.

"Actually, I'd like to ask you out for a coffee so we could get to know each other when you're not working."

She blushes and lowers her eyes. There's no fluttering eyelashes. No cloying coyness.

"Yes, I'd like that," she says.

"I live in Chinatown but I could meet you around here if there's somewhere with good coffee," I offer.

"The Trattoria upstairs is good, but I actually live near Washington Square Park," she says. "Do you know Dregs on Thompson Street? They have really good coffee."

"I don't, but I'll find it. Weather forecast is nice and I have a bunch of neighbor's dogs to walk." Acting isn't a steady gig and The Famous Guy keeps doing things like parting ways with big franchises, which may limit my future gigs even more. Always good to have something to fall back on. "If you don't mind walking, we could grab coffees to go, walk and talk?"

As sweet and genuine as Briar's smile was after the scene, Char's is a thousand times sweeter. "I have a Staffy. Could I bring her?"

She's a dog person. That was always a bone of contention between me and Amber, who insisted on only having cats.

"That would be great." Around us, the lights dim and the music rises to a level that will make casual conversation a challenge. "I guess the club's opening."

Char nods. "Sorry, I've got to go upstairs. I'm scheduled for a scene at nine thirty."

I hold out my hand. "Pleasure to meet you."

"You, too, Ian. When did you want to get that coffee?"

"Tomorrow."

She grins shyly. "That would be great."

"Eleven too early?"

She shakes her head.

"See you tomorrow at eleven at Dregs. Anything comes up, call me. Your friend Brenna has my number."

I'd offer her my number, but I'm assuming the house submissives don't have their phones in the club, either. There's certainly nowhere in the corset and tiny panties to hide a phone. Communicating through Brenna's tattoo parlor seems safe and neither of us has to remember a phone number.

Char nods. "She has mine, too. It's been so nice to meet you."

Goodbyes said, we should step away from each other. Neither of us move. I still have Char's hand clasped in mine. When she doesn't withdraw it, I stroke her knuckles with my thumb.

She sucks her lower lip between her teeth.

My smile's so wide, my cheeks ache, but I don't try to suppress it.

"I'll see you tomorrow, Char."

She nods, her cheeks flushing as pink as the lip she releases.

"I'll see you then," she murmurs, barely audible over the music.

Neither of us move away.

"You're going to be late," I say, teasing just a little.

"I shouldn't be late." A hint of mischief creeps into her smile. "I wouldn't want to get a punishment."

Fuck. Me.

"Save that for tomorrow," I say, my voice dropping lower than the music's bass line. "I want that honor."

Her eyes flash and she slowly pulls her hand out of mine. "Would being ten minutes late earn me a punishment?"

I nod. "I value punctuality."

"See you tomorrow, Ian. At eleven-ten." She curtsies and runs off toward the elevator as fast as she can manage on the stilettos.

I watch her until the elevator doors close, hiding her brilliant grin and sparkling eyes. When I finally tear myself away, I take the fresh drink from the bartender and make my way slowly back to the table.

I don't stay long afterwards. Just long enough for a dance with Brenna and another with a black-haired, blue-eyed beauty named Fleur who despite being just as eye-catching as Char doesn't light the same fire in my belly. I'm home so early that King, my Irish Setter, isn't even waiting for me at the door. After I give him a night-time brush and cuddle, I settle into bed. It's not even midnight yet; definitely the earliest I've ever been home from a nightclub. But it's the best night I've had in a long time.

So good I don't even need to jack off before my eyelids get heavy. My well is brimming and my heart's full of promise.

[To be continued . . .]

a notorious tail — part 3

MASTER IAN AND BRIAR ROSE - BRENNA

AM I LYING IN WAIT?

No, of course not. As my Sir would say, that's beneath me.

But by the Benevolence, I cannot wait to see Briar's face.

Cappa sidles over to where I'm standing at the Trattoria buffet, a step behind my Sir as he loads our plates. Off to my right, that megawatt smile breaks out as Char leans over to whisper something to Ian.

Ian, who looks at Char the way Logan looks at Emily, the way I sometimes catch Mac looking at me. Char's more reserved, but when Ian cuts a piece of his quiche and offers it to her, she glows.

Tonight's only the third time Ian's been to the club, and it's for an open night at the Trattoria, so members mingle freely with non-members, although the guest list is heavily vetted. But Char's told me that Ian's going to put in an application for membership after tonight. She and I are already planning to finagle Master Sean into sponsoring Ian. They're close in temperament and Char's told me Ian cannot get enough of pony play, now that he's discovered it. Master Sean can show Ian the literal ropes.

I'm not sure whether Char will continue to be a house submissive or if she'll have to approach Chairman Chess and hope for the kind of deal he offered me, but if Char's not wearing a second collar by the time Ian's membership is approved, I'll eat Mac's shorts.

That's not why I'm lurking like a freaking darkmantle, though.

Ian's let his natural hair color show tonight. He's not wearing blue contacts. Yes, he still looks a lot like The Famous Guy, as Ian calls him. But without the dye and contacts, the eye's less easily fooled. It's clear they're not the same person.

"She's going to shit a brick, isn't she?" Cappa murmurs to me, following my line of sight.

"Oh, yeah."

He grins and heads back to sit with Emmy and Logan, a skip in his step.

When Mac finishes picking food—and dayum if he doesn't get all my faves, I love my Sir—I drag him to the table next to Char and Ian's and plonk down so I'm facing the door.

Mac screws up his face at me. "Not that I don't value our one-on-one time, girl, but is there a reason we're not sitting with Logan and Emily? Still space at their table."

"I'd rather sit here, if you don't mind, Sir."

The only seats left at Emmy and Logan's table look out into the conservatory. I won't see Briar's face when she comes in and gets an eyeful of Ian. They can spare us this once.

"Somethin' you're not telling me, girl?" Mac asks as I dive into the spicy noodles he's picked.

"Why would you think that, Sir?"

"Because I've seen that grin before and I know you're up to no good. Spill, girl."

I twirl my fork in my noodles while I consider how to admit my deviousness without earning a punishment. Mac's punishments are really not fun.

"Hypothetically," I begin.

Mac grumbles.

"Okay, it's not very hypothetical. I know you've noticed how much Ian looks like a certain famous person."

Mac grunts. "I've noticed."

"After he got his tattoo, I invited him to Blunts and introduced him to a bunch of the house subs."

"I see," Mac says slowly. "Lemme guess. You introduced him as the other fella."

"I let them assume."

"Still lying, girl."

"I prefer to think of it as obfuscation."

"Call it whatever you want. Lying's lying. You know what that gets you."

I wince. "It's the Delrin, isn't it?"

"Uh-huh."

Fuck.

Then Briar walks through the restaurant door. She's talking with her groupie, Tamsin. It takes her a minute to look around the Trattoria and spot him.

Her jaw nearly hits the floor.

Oh, yes. Yes-yes-yes. She's been telling everyone who would listen about her "scene with a celebrity." The tale gets taller every time she tells it. Last I heard her telling Annabelle, The Famous Guy picked her out of a crowd of submissives and asked her to scene with him by bowing so low, his red cape swept the floor at her feet.

None of us have corrected her. We heard Ian tell her the truth. Her delusions are of her own making.

After the initial shock, she snaps her mouth closed. Her face freezes. She lifts her chin and stalks over to the buffet line, looking everywhere but at Char and Ian.

Ian's so besotted with Char, I don't think he even notices.

But Char does. She winks at me before she turns her adoring gaze back to Ian.

Worth. Every. Stroke.

[The End]

25

FOUR

*an adventurous
tail*

DADDY JACK AND SAMMI - SAMMI

"SAMMI! Come down here and explain yourself."

Uh-oh.

I stash my burner phone in my nightstand, check in the bathroom mirror to make sure I'm not wearing any sign of guilt, run my fingers through my hair so it sticks up the way Daddy likes, and trot downstairs.

"Hi, Daddy! I didn't hear you come in."

My daddy leans against the granite kitchen counter. He fits perfectly in the modern kitchen with its stainless-steel appliances and glossy cabinetry. He's wearing one of his tailored suits; his hair is combed back in a black wing even more glossy than the cabinets; his square jaw is so recently shaven he doesn't even have a five o'clock shadow. He looks every inch the high-powered surgeon.

I'm barefoot and wearing a bright yellow onesie.

He opens his arms and I run to him. He smells so good. Clean linen and black pepper and pachouli. He must have showered after he finished his rounds. I burrow into his chest and soak up my daddy.

"You smell good."

"You sound guilty. What is Project Harry?"

Emily's daddy is a narc. She's the only one of us who refused to get a secret phone; he must have seen our plans on her phone and sold us out.

"We're just planning an outing."

"What sort of outing?"

I've talked myself into a corner. I should have thought this out better.

"We, um, wanted to see some baby animals."

"At the zoo? We just went last month. I don't think the bunnies are quite ready to see you again."

I might have squeezed them too hard. They're not like my stuffies.

"This is upstate. Emmy wanted to combine it with a trip to see her mom."

There. Ha. Serves Logan right.

"Emmy's mother lives in Syracuse. That's really far upstate, baby. Like four hours. How far were you planning on going?"

This is why I shouldn't be in charge!

"Uh, I don't know. We're just planning things right now."

"Is there somewhere specific you want to go?"

I can't tell him the name of the place that Cynnie told us about where the evil scientists are torturing Harry. He'll look it up and realize it's not a petting zoo or farm. "We're still looking for places."

"Do you want daddy to help you look?"

Cornered! Help!

"Yummy and Cynnie are in charge of picking places."

Daddy gives me a long look. How am I supposed to get away with anything when he looks at me with those dark, knowing eyes?

"Hm. I'll talk with Bravo and Max."

"They might be keeping it a surprise!" I wail. "You'll spoil the surprise."

He ruffles my hair with a big, warm hand. "Okay, I don't want to spoil the surprise. When you have a better idea of places, tell me and we'll figure out how to get there. I know Logan and Emmy take the train up to Syracuse when they go to see her mother. I'd rather drive since we have your entertainment center in the car."

I pout. I love trains. We took a train up to Niagara Falls for Logan and Emmy's collaring ceremony; it was so much fun. Yummy and I played hide and seek all through the train and no one ever found me.

Daddy flicks my lower lip with his thumb before leaning in to give me a kiss. I sag against his hard, long body. I love Daddy's kisses. There is a hit of heady mint from the peppermint tea he likes and underneath a dark, rich taste that's all Daddy. Like the steak with béarnaise sauce we make together. The béarnaise sauce is creamy with a counterpoint of acidity and licorice. Then the rich meatiness of the steak hits.

That's Daddy. On the outside, he's responsible and smooth and civilized. On the inside, he's dark and dirty and wild. He thrives on giving me the most evil punishments. He goes on weekend retreats with Bravo and his friend Henry. When I ask what they're doing, he says they're hunting or fishing, but they never bring back any game. I thought he might be a secret agent until I met Cynnie's daddy's friend De Leon, who really is a secret agent. He didn't recognize Daddy and all secret agents know each other. They have special handshakes and stuff. That's what my friend Aleksei says and he should know. His grandparents were Russian.

"You ready to make dinner with me?" Daddy asks when he breaks the kiss after lots of nibbles at my lower lip that make my head spin.

I nod. "Can we make pasta together like the other night?"

Daddy smiles. "You liked that, huh?"

"Yes!"

I gave Daddy a pasta machine for his birthday, a really nice one that Miss Ginger helped me pick out, all gleaming copper and steel. He let me crank the handle while he fed the dough through the rollers and it came out perfect! It tasted so much better than pasta from the store that I only want homemade pasta from now on.

He kisses my forehead. "You get the eggs and flour while I get the machine out and we'll make Tagliatelle all'Amatriciana, since we have that beautiful pancetta from the deli."

"Yes, Daddy."

He gives me another kiss—I love Daddy's kisses so much—before he moves away, stripping off his suit jacket and grabbing two aprons off the hooks near the fridge. He wraps one apron around his lean hips and slings the other around my neck.

Grinning from all the good attention, and a little from getting one over on Daddy, I pull the apron down over my onesie.

I huddle around Emily's puzzle table with Emily, Yummy, Cynnie, Aggie, and Brenna. Brenna's only an honorary member of the Littles' Army, since she's not a little. But she's one of us in every other way and she can keep a secret like nobody's business.

"I don't want to be critical," Brenna says, tracing her finger over the map Cynnie's brought. Because every good rescue mission needs a map. "But I feel I should point out two things. First, you need somewhere for Harry to go after you rescue him—"

"He's coming to live with me!" I protest. That's always been the cornerstone of the plan.

Brenna scratches her pile of blue dreadlocks. "Okay, first, you need a backup location for where Harry's going after you rescue him. Just in case your place doesn't work out, Sammi."

I cross my arms over my chest. There's no reason my place won't work out. Daddy said I could have a pet this year if I was responsible enough, just like Emmy got a kitty and Aggie got a puppy. I've been super-responsible. For weeks! Since Daddy Max made us our own app, I even remember to drink all my water every day. I only earned two dings this week and one really wasn't my fault. Neither of them were, actually. Daddy didn't see it that way, but even he admits that he's wrong sometimes.

"Uh-huh," Brenna continues, "second, I just want to put on the table that if you don't come clean to your daddies about what you're really doing, they're going to punish the fuck out of you."

"But we can't just leave Harry there," Cynnie says softly. "They're doing *experiments* on him. They scare him just to test the levels of chloride in his blood. They're *torturing* him. Lindy told Oppa so."

"See?" I say to Brenna. "We have to rescue Harry."

"I'm not arguing with the mission," Brenna responds. "Operation Rescue Harry is imperative. I just think you need to tweak the design. Your daddies would probably agree to help if you told them, you know."

I shake my head. The plans of the Littles' Army must stay secret. The daddies would definitely disband us if they knew.

"What if we asked Master Mac to supervise the field trip? The daddies could do daddy things instead," Cynnie suggests.

Yummy sniggers. "They could go bowling."

"Bowling? I want to go bowling!" I bounce up and down on my crossed legs. Bowling's so much fun, especially when Daddy helps me bowl. Daddy's super-competitive and does everything well, but I beat him at bowling when he helps me.

"We can plan a bowling day next, Sammi," Emily says. "I don't think Master Mac would let us bring Harry home with us."

"You've got that right." Brenna chuckles. "He'd rat you out to your daddies before we were even out of the city limits."

"What about your friend Daisy?" I ask Emily. "Would she help?"

Emily nods. "Probably, but she's in Mexico on a shoot. She won't be back for another week. We can't leave Harry that long if he's being tortured."

We all get the same idea at the same time and turn to look at Brenna.

She holds up her palms. "Oh, no. Not a chance. I will help you liberate Harry but I'm not supervising the rescue mission on my own. You get at least one of your daddies to come or nothing. That's the deal. Besides, I don't drive and someone needs to drive the getaway car."

"I can drive," Emily protests. "We'd need to rent a car since mine's in Syracuse, but I can drive it."

"Emmy, we're rescuing a *fainting mini-goat*. It's a living, stinking stuffie. You're going to be deep in littlespace the whole time and you know it. You shouldn't be driving."

Emily makes a face at Brenna but doesn't argue.

"I think Oppa would do it," Cynnie offers. "He was really upset about Harry after Lindy told him. He talked about it all night. I think he might be planning something himself. I got these schematics off his computer."

We "ooo" collectively.

"You'll ask him?" Emmy asks Cynnie.

Cynnie nods, her straight black hair, streaked with purple, swinging against her cheeks.

"What if he rats us out to the other daddies, though?" I ask.

Cynnie shrugs. "I could ask him to Hive Swear before I told him. That's only for the most secret, most important stuff—"

"Harry's *life* is at stake!" I insist.

"I know, I know," Cynnie says. "Okay, I'll ask him to Hive Swear first."

"That's a plan," Brenna says. "Now, about location B."

"We're not going to need location B," I tell her. "Daddy said I could have a pet like Sable and Kublai Khan."

"But Sammi, Sable is a cat and Khan is a dog. I'm really confident Jack thought you'd want a kitty or a puppy or even a goldfish, not a fainting mini-goat."

"But I love him," I wail. I've loved Harry since Cynnie put his picture in the group chat. I looked into those weird, reptilian eyes and knew he was my goaty soul-mate.

"Look, I have an idea. It's a long shot, but after Emmy did all that research on the history of Blunts and found out about Madame

Glass's menagerie . . . well, it gave me an idea. We *have* to ask Chairman Chess, though. We cannot just show up at Blunts with a mini-goat. This is beyond punishment. He'd convert one of the dungeons into a little jail, toss you all in, and throw away the key. I'm not joking."

Yummy and I trade glances. Getting locked up with our daddies out on Spin Island was crazy fun. As long as Daddy is locked up with me . . .

"Sammi, I see that look. No. I'm not doing it. No. I owe Chairman Chess. I'm not showing up with a clowder of littles and a goat. Omigod, that sounds like the beginning of a bad joke." Brenna claps her hand to her forehead.

"A daddy, a little, and Harry the fainting mini-goat walk into a bar," I quip.

Everyone around the table giggles.

"I'll come with you to ask Chairman Chess," Emily volunteers. "If he agrees to Harry, I have an idea for a real stable off the Stables. We could have bunnies, too. I really want bunnies. Like those bunnies in Niagara Falls. We could have a group of therapy bunnies based at Blunts."

Brenna massages her forehead like she has a headache. "Okay, that's the plan. Emily and I will approach Chess tomorrow. Cynnie will get Max on board. Max can drive the getaway car. Operation Rescue Harry the Fainting Mini-Goat is a go."

I stick my hand in the middle of the table, over the map. Four hands slap down on top of mine. After a moment, Brenna slaps her hand on top of the pile.

"Pooyah! Littles' Army!"

I know the moment Cynnie's daddy betrays us. My phone lights up like a Christmas tree.

Daddy: You and I are going to have a very serious conversation when I get home.

Daddy: I can't believe you've been keeping this from me.

Daddy: Answer me, Sammi.

But-but-but he hasn't asked me a question!

I turn off my phone, grab my blankie and Churchill the Walrus, and hide in the cage in Daddy's closet. He usually punishes me in the cage and when I'm being punished I hate the cage. But Daddy told me if I was ever really scared or if I thought someone was trying to break into the house, I could hide in the cage until he came and got me.

Today seems like a good day to hide in the cage.

I forget to take a bottle of water with me and after a little while, I get really thirsty. But I'm nice and safe in the cage with blankie and Churchill, so I stay put and suck on my thumb to wet my dry mouth.

I guess I fall asleep, which isn't hard to do because the cage floor is padded and Churchill's tummy makes a good pillow and I fall asleep easily when I suck my thumb even though I don't do it much anymore after Daddy told me it was hurting my teeth and bought me a paci.

When I wake up, the bedroom's dark. There's a little light from the bathroom safety light. It silvers Daddy's hair and outlines his broad shoulders as he sits in a chair in front of the closet.

"Daddy?"

He starts, lifting his chin from his chest. He rubs his hands over his face and sits forward, resting his elbows on his knees.

"Formal protocol, Sammi. You're in trouble."

My throat thickens. I haven't been in formal protocol-level trouble in a long time. I sit up in the cage and push blankie away. Formal protocol means I have to think big. "Yes, Sir."

"Did you get in the cage because I scared you or for another reason?"

"Because I was scared."

"Because you know you did serious wrong in planning to steal a goat?"

I try to blink back the wetness welling in my eyes. "It's not *stealing*. They're doing experiments on him and PETA is trying to rescue him and everything but they were kept away by a bad policeman who is getting paid off by the evil scientists."

Daddy blows out a long breath. "Okay, Sammi. I agree with what you're trying to do. I don't want the mini-goat experimented on, either, but you can't just steal a goat. Logan's gotten the club's lawyer involved. We'll handle it through legal channels."

"And bring Harry home?" I ask hopefully.

"What?"

"When you get Harry away from the evil scientists, he'll come and live with us?"

Daddy rubs his hands over his face again. "Sammi."

"Please, Sir? Please, you said I could have a pet like Emmy and Aggie."

"I did," Daddy says slowly. "I thought you'd want something at least semi-domesticated."

"Goats are domesticated."

"I don't think the condo association will see it that way. Okay, baby boy. Formal protocol's over. Come give me a hug. You're still getting a punishment for keeping secrets but I see your heart was in the right place. Come here to me."

I shove the cage door open with a clang and scramble out. Daddy leans down and I push myself up into his arms. He settles me on his lap and hugs me tight.

"I love you, Daddy."

"I love you, too, boo-boo. You bring your gremlin energy into my life and I love every minute of it, even when you make me *pazzo*."

I bury my face in Daddy's warm neck. His scent is tart with sweat. Did he run home? I thought he was sleeping when I woke up. Was he sweating in his sleep?

"You're sweaty," I mutter into the fine wool covering his shoulder.

"It's been a nerve-wracking day."

"Were there lots of hurt kids?"

"No, four routine procedures. My nerves have been shredded by the plots of littles that would have landed them in some podunk prison upstate. Why didn't you tell me about Harry?"

"I wanted to rescue him myself and bring him home to live with us. He's my soul-mate."

Daddy chuckles. "I thought I was your soul-mate?"

"He's my *goaty* soul-mate."

"I see. You can visit your goaty soul-mate on Mondays, Wednesdays, and Fridays when you have that big gap between classes. The club's not far from school."

"Can't Harry live with us? Please, Daddy. I'll do all the right things. I'll take care of him—"

"Sammi, no. Goats need space to run and play. And eat. And poop. Logan's club has agreed that if we can get custody of Harry, they'll house him there. Something about expanding the Stables and having bunnies and a historical menagerie, I don't know. It all got confused in the goat-napping."

"It wasn't a goat-napping. We're the Mini-Goat Liberation League."

Daddy snorts. "Mac is having T-shirts made. Littles' Army? Hm. I'll have him put Mini-Goat Liberation League on the back."

"In pink *and* baby blue?"

"Yes, in pink and baby blue. You're not getting out of the punishment, Sammi. I know what you're trying to do. Making me laugh will not make me forget the day I've had *or* that you turned off your phone and ignored me. I know I scared you and I've told you before you can hide in the cage if you need to, but I wish you'd responded to my text before you did. I've been worried, boo-boo. I had to check the monitors to make sure you were okay and when I saw you'd gotten in the cage I could barely think about anything else until the end of my shift."

"I wasn't trying to get out of my punishment. I was just trying to make you less sweaty. I'm sorry I made you worry, though."

He rubs his hand up and down my back. I'm still wearing the sweatshirt and jeans I wore to class. I'd just gotten home and unpacked my school bag when Cynnie's daddy betrayed us.

I know the Littles' Army's next op is bowling, but after that, I think we need to plan the Mini-Goat's Revenge on Daddy Max. Betrayal cannot be tolerated.

"What punishment do you think is fitting for keeping secrets from daddy, little boy?"

"A hundred lines?" I suggest hopefully.

"Think again."

"Two hundred lines?"

"Sammi, you know the rule. No keeping secrets. I can't help my boy with things I don't know about. This whole Littles' Army and the Great Mini-Goat Rescue is a huge secret. You even had a meeting to plan it when you were supposed to be watching a movie at Logan's—"

"We *did* watch a movie. I told you about it, remember? It was really good except that it should have been a prince rather than a princess. There are too few princes in movies these days."

"I think that's probably because there were too many princes in movies previously. Sammi, stop trying to divert me. Punishment."

I sigh. Daddy's very focused and my efforts to avoid punishments are usually unsuccessful, but a boy has to try.

"Cock cage?" I ask, knowing what's coming.

"Cock cage. And ice."

I wince. Ice is cold.

"I don't like ice."

"I know you don't. That's the idea of punishment, Sammi. You're not supposed to like it. If you're a good boy, you can have a funishment the day after tomorrow. But today, it's ice and the cock cage and no orgasms until tomorrow night."

I sigh deeply and drop my forehead against his chest. "I'm sad."

He strokes my hair. "I know. And I always want you to tell me how you feel. But you're not getting out of this. No secrets, Sammi. That's the rule. You broke the rule."

I nod and rub my cheek against his jacket. "Now?"

"Yes. Let's get the ice done and cage on. Then I'll make dinner while you have some time in your playpen to relax."

"Can I have blankie and Churchill with me?"

"Of course."

He helps me off his lap, then gathers my blanket and stuffie. I undress and hand him my clothes, which he helps me fold and put away. Daddy always wants me to go into punishments nakey. He says it helps me get into the right mindset. Since the cock cage is Daddy's favorite punishment, being nakey helps me go into the punishment with my winkie small because you do not want a swollen winkie going into a cock cage. All the ouch.

Daddy drapes my blankie around me while he changes from the suit he wore to the hospital.

"Go use the toilet while I get the ice ready, Sammi," Daddy says as he pulls on jeans and a soft sweatshirt that says, "Cornell Crew."

"Don't need," I say before I think it through.

Daddy frowns. "You were asleep for an hour and in the cage for an hour before that. Give me your phone."

Wincing, I bring it to him.

He powers it on, opens it, and thumbs to the app Benedict Daddy made for us.

"Sammi." He blows out a breath. "Go get your water bottle. I want you to drink eight ounces before we get started. You haven't had anything to drink in hours."

"I didn't want to come out of the cage," I mutter as I retrieve my bright, superhero water bottle and tip it up to my mouth.

"I understand you wanting the safety of the cage but not at the expense of your heath, boo-boo. Would it help if I hooked up a water bottle in the cage?"

I take a breath and answer him before slurping down more water. "Yes, please, Daddy."

He strokes my head before he takes my hand and leads me downstairs. I usually like hearing the slap-slap of Daddy's bare feet on the wood floors. That sound means he's home and has taken his shoes off for daddy-boy time. But today it's not a very good sound.

I hate ice.

"I want you up on the table for this," Daddy tells me as we cross the hallway and head into the open-plan dining room and kitchen. "Get the pad and the lube and clear off the table."

I nod since I'm still drinking my water. Daddy heads into the kitchen while I go to the cupboard where we keep scene supplies. Punishment means I'll be uncomfortable, but not injured, as Daddy's told me a hundred times. My back appreciates the difference, as I take out a thick cushion with a towel cover and put it on the table. I take the candles, glass centerpiece, salt and pepper shakers, and napkins off the heavy, wood dining table and put them on a shelf in the closet.

Daddy's rummaging around in the freezer, which is definitely bad news for my bottom. If he was just getting ice, he'd be using the ice cube maker on the door. I'm pretty sure I know what's coming.

He takes out a long, silicone mold and puts it on the counter.

I wasn't wrong. I sigh.

"I hear you, little boy."

"I hate the ice dildo, Daddy."

"Mmm. You always struggle not to come when I fuck you with it, so I think it's more of a love-hate relationship."

I scowl at it as I climb up onto the table and position myself on the cushion.

"Diaper position. Hold behind your knees and spread your legs. Show me everything that belongs to daddy."

I love being fucked in diaper position because Daddy hits my P-spot just right and plays with my cock and balls while he's fucking me. That's the only reason I struggle not to come during punishments. Nothing to do with the ice dildo, which is horrible-horribler-horriblest.

Daddy opens the mold and slides the long, flat-bottomed tube of ice into a bowl. He tosses in a baggie and adds ice cubes to make an ice pack, then brings the instruments of torture over to the table.

"Check in, little boy. How are you doing?"

"Sad," I tell him, pouting up at him from between my knees.

"Sad with shades of remorseful or sad with an edge of defiance?"

"The first one."

"Maybe this will make you feel better." He takes his phone out of his pocket, taps for a moment, and then turns it so I can see the screen.

It's a text message from Daddy Logan:

Goat's ours. For better or worse.

I grin at Daddy.

"If you and your team of troublemakers had brought this to us in the first place, we'd have figured it out without the potential for incarceration."

"I just wanted to be Harry's hero."

Daddy smiles as he runs his warm palm down my chest and over my tummy. I don't have the six pack Daddy has, but working out with him has made my tummy flat and firm.

"Will you settle for being my hero?" Daddy asks.

I nod eagerly. "Heroes don't get punished."

"Nice try. Heroes who break the rules get punished. Fortunately, my little hero's only getting punished by his daddy instead of the long arm of the law. Next time you consider keeping secrets from daddy, I want you to remember this."

He takes the baggie out of the bowl and drapes it over my pubic bone. I wince and shiver as the cold coats my winkie and seeps down over my balls, which contract to the size of grapes. I can't see anything under the ice pack, but I'm sure all my important bits have climbed right up inside my stomach, where a fierce ache starts.

"Cold," I hiss at Daddy.

"Really?" He touches the ice pack with his fingertips, moving it around so it comes into contact with everything between my legs. "Yes, it seems that way."

"I think the ice pack is enough punishment," I say, but it's only a suggestion, because defying daddy ends badly for me. "It was only a little secret."

"So there's no confusion in the future, Sammi, kidnapping a goat is not a little secret. It's a great, big, whopping secret. As is the formation of a Littles' Army with your friends. Logan, Warrin, Bravo, Max, Mac, and I do not approve."

"Master Mac does. You said he was getting us T-shirts."

Daddy grumbles but he must realize I have a point because he picks up the lube and drizzles it over his fingers. He shifts the ice pack out of the way and rims my hole. His eyes darken as he takes me in, doubled up on the table with my legs in the air, completely exposed to him. One slick fingertip breaches me, then another, opening me slowly. He works his fingers in and out, spreading the lube, adding more when he feels a little friction, until I must be dripping.

Then he picks up the ice dildo and presses the tip to my hole.

I squeak at the sting. He's trained me to hold position, but it's so hard as every muscle in my body tenses, wanting to get away from the horrible, bitter bite at that sensitive opening. The ache spreads front and back and I have to grip my knees to hold myself in place.

"Please, Daddy, no more," I beg. Begging's allowed, even when I'm being punished.

"Mm, a little more. Do you keep secrets from daddy, Sammi?"

"No, Daddy. No secrets."

He works the dildo in and the sting spreads up into my bottom, making me shiver all over.

"Not even small secrets, Sammi. Not that goat-napping is a small secret, but the rule is you tell daddy everything. Remember?"

"Yes, Daddy. I'll remember better in the future."

He works the dildo in and out until half of its gleaming length is buried in my bottom and I'm feeling the achy cold all the way up through my guts.

"Daddy, please, it's making my tummy hurt."

Daddy nods and takes the ice pack off my groin but doesn't take the Spear of Ice out of my bottom.

"Daddy," I whine.

He chuckles. "Is it this that's giving you a tummy ache, little boy?" he asks, wiggling the Ice Lance.

"Yes!"

"Mm-hmm. Will you keep secrets from daddy?"

"No! Never!"

He pumps the rod in and out. A cold gush soaks the pad underneath me. I desperately try to hold position but my feet kick at the ache and my buttocks clench, which only brings more of my poor, flinching skin in contact with the freezing-fire.

"Little more. Be good for me, Sammi."

"I'm trying, Daddy!"

He tortures me for another minute and then withdraws the horrible-horribler-horriblest thing. It leaves a weird, warm trail in its wake as it withdraws.

I sigh and tuck my head up between my knees so I can wipe my eyes with my thumbs. "Thank you for taking it out, Daddy."

"You're welcome, little boy. Your hole is very red."

"And cold! And stingy!"

"Will you keep secrets again?"

"No. Never. I promise."

"Good boy. Stay in position for me while I put the cage on you."

I wiggle a little on the damp pad but make sure to hold my legs open so he can close the metal over my poor, shriveled parts. I didn't see what cage he brought out. Daddy has a terrifying selection. But when just smooth metal touches me, I sigh with relief. It's one of the normal cages, not a cage with teeth, so Daddy must not be too angry with me.

Once he clicks the locks on the cage, I relax and start to lower my legs.

"No, stay in position. I want that little, red hole."

I wiggle happily, tilting my hips into a better position. Getting fucked when I can't come isn't as fun as when I can, but it's still good. It's still Daddy fucking me.

He opens his jeans and takes himself out. Daddy has the nicest cock, which I love to look at. I'd never been with a man with his olive skin tone before Daddy. His cock flushes purple when he's aroused and even when I'm being punished, all I want to do is admire him.

"Please can I see?"

Daddy chuckles. "Yes, pup."

He fists himself and shows off, stroking slowly so the skin pulls and rolls and flushes an even deeper color.

"You're so beautiful, Daddy."

"Thank you, boy. You're beautiful, too. Never more beautiful than when you're submitting to me." He squeezes a little lube onto his tip and works it down with easy strokes. "Ready?"

I nod eagerly.

"Let go of your legs and grab the edge of the table."

When I do, Daddy sets a warm, firm hand on my thigh to hold one leg open. He rubs his tip all around my hole. His cockhead feels feverishly hot after the ice and I moan at the sensation. After he guides his head into me, he plants his hand on my other knee and holds me open as he sinks into me with a long groan.

"Feels so strange," he grunts.

It feels strange to me, too. Numb and tingly, like my butthole has somehow fallen asleep. But it gets better with each stroke as his hot skin and the friction warm me up.

He quickly settles into his pace, hard and deep, snapping his hips at the end of each stroke, the way we both like. The ache in my belly becomes something warm and swirly instead of cold and crampy. I look up at my daddy, pumping over me, his usual calm expression peeling back into bared teeth and burning eyes. I love watching Daddy's wildness come out. He only shows it to me. Only in these moments when he lets himself go. He's not the competent surgeon. He's not the controlled Dom. He's my daddy and in these moments, he's capable of anything.

"Good boy, Sammi." He leans over and kisses me, nipping at my lower lip. When he pushes up, he leaves one hand circling my throat, just above my day collar. His long, strong, skilled fingers massage the tendon until my head begins to spin.

"I'm going to come in you, boy. I'm going to fill up this hole, hot and full. I know it feels good. You do not have permission to come."

"Yes, Daddy." I want to be good for him now. I know I'm a handful and Daddy says he likes the challenge but even I know when enough is enough.

It's hard, though, when every thrust pushes bright sparks of sensation up my spine. My asshole's finally thawed and it's so, so sensitive. I feel like I could come if he just blew on my cock, which is throbbing in its metal confines. His pace picks up, a fluid pounding, and I cling to the edge of the table to keep in place.

Daddy growls, deep and low, something he never, ever docs except when he's close. I whimper at the sound. It makes my tummy churn with heat. Each breath catches in my chest.

"Yes, Daddy, please come in me."

He groans, his head snapping back as his whole body flexes. He bears down into me, shoving deep, his chest coming down onto my knees. He pins me hard to the table as his hips piston, pumping his heat deep into me.

Despite the constriction of the cage, relief shoots through me with the impact of Daddy's cock on my prostate. It's not a full orgasm, but it feels so, so good to come with him.

Daddy kisses me, teasing my upper lip with his tongue. When he lifts up off me, a shining string stretches between his thigh and the cage.

"Sammi, did you come?"

"A teeny-tiny amount."

"Like the teeny-tiny goat we now have." Daddy throws back his head and laughs. "What am I going to do with you?"

"Love me!"

He leans over and rubs noses with me. "Yes, my boy. I love you. I can't imagine loving anyone more."

I release the table, flex my aching fingers, and reach for him. He leans over me so I can hug him hard.

"You'll love Harry, too?"

He shakes his head as he looks down at me, his eyes tranquil, face relaxed. "I'll do my best to love Harry, too. And if I can't, I know you'll love him enough for both of us, my boy."

I will. No goat will ever be as well-loved as Harry the fainting mini-goat.

[The End]

an impecunious tail – part 1

BLUNTS HOUSE SUBMISSIVES – FLEUR

I LOOK around the train station again for a tall figure cutting through the crowds toward me.

Lots of scurrying commuters. No way-past-fashionably late Dom.

I check my phone. My last five messages are still showing as unread.

Damn him.

I stride over to a food kiosk, dragging my huge suitcase, backpack, and handbag, order pumpkin spice coffee with whipped cream, a sandwich, and in a moment of furious defiance, not one but two donuts.

While I wait for my food, I start shaking. What if he shows up now? What if he catches the train at the last minute and sees what I've ordered?

I check my phone again. Still delivered but not read.

The kid behind the kiosk counter gives me an appreciative look as he makes my coffee. "Where are you headed?"

"Upstate," I tell him, trying not to let anger and hurt spill into my tone. He's just trying to be nice. If I was five years younger and not about to be late for my train, I'd flirt a little.

He hands me my order and opens his mouth for more gentle flirtation.

I give him a smile, which is probably ghoulish with my drawn cheeks and black lipstick. "Sorry, I've got to run."

And I really do. I've waited for Nigel way too long.

Sweating from dragging my bags down the long platform and up the steps into my carriage, I flop into my seat. My scalp prickles under my wig. With a last glance out of the window at the platform, I tug the hairpins holding the wig in place and pull it off, folding it in my lap.

I run my hands through my natural, black waves. Nigel permits my black makeup, but he doesn't like me looking "too goth." When we're out together in public, I wear the auburn wig he prefers.

I've dressed to please him today—like every day—and all it's gotten me is an itchy scalp.

I put my wig away in my handbag and pull out my phone and paperback book. Nigel had a window seat, which is empty. I move over into it and fold down the little table built into the arm of the chair.

A shadow falls over me; I freeze.

The donuts are in the paper bag at my feet. If I don't open it, maybe he won't notice them.

"Ticket please, miss," a man says.

I look up, taking in his uniform. With a relieved smile, I dig out my ticket and offer it to him. He scans it and nods at me before moving on.

I set up my coffee and meal on the table, check my phone—still unread—and open my paperback. I bring it to my nose for a surreptitious sniff. I love the smell of books. For a long time, they were locked boxes to me. I loved them even when they were vaults; I loved the look and feel of them. After I finally learned to read in middle school, I had so much ground to make up. Books became my best friends.

They never judged me like some of my teachers and classmates did. They just surrendered their knowledge with a whisper of worn paper and the smell of vanilla.

Books were my first lesson in submission.

My phone pings just as I take out my bookmark and start to read.

Nigel: Baby, I can't leave work. We'll go to the next one. I'll make it up to you.

I shake my head at my phone. He just assumes I won't go without him. A few years ago, I wouldn't have. I'd have waited on the platform for him and trudged home with my tail between my legs and tears drying on my cheeks when he didn't show.

At the end of the day, the only person you answer to, is you.

Master Javier's words ring in my ears. He and Master Logan were the first Doms to notice that I was so dependent on my Dom's approval that I couldn't make decisions. They worked with me for a long time to help me understand the difference between submission and dependence. Neither of them wanted me for their own, but I'll always be grateful to both of them.

As always, when I have grateful thoughts, I flip my phone over to my submission diary, note my gratitude, and then shoot a text to Master Javier.

Thank you for helping me find myself.

He answers within a few seconds, the way he always does.

Master J: You're very welcome, my dear. Enjoy your time off. I'll miss you tomorrow. I'd like a rain check on Wednesday.

I smile at his message.

Wednesday is yours, sir.

I thumb back to Nigel's message. I tap my fingernails on my phone screen for a minute, then message him back.

Sorry you're not coming. I'll see you when I get back.

I tuck my phone away, take a sip of coffee and a big bite of donut, and open my book.

"I'm sorry, miss," the man behind the hotel counter says. "I'll need a new credit card for the room. This one's been canceled."

I start digging in my bag automatically. I don't have a credit card of my own—one of the conditions of Masters Franco and Cris helping get back on my feet financially was that I stop using credit cards—but I have the Blunts card that all house submissives are issued for emergencies.

"I-I'm sorry," I say to the clerk as I hand over the black card. "Did you say the card's been canceled?"

He nods. "The card holder called a few hours ago and canceled all charges to the card."

I close my mouth with a snap.

"That's all set, miss," the clerk says, handing me back the card. "Don't see many of those."

I try to smile as I tuck the card away. Nigel canceled his card. While I was on the train, reading and eating my donuts, he canceled his goddamn card. Knowing I don't have a credit card of my own. He doesn't know about the Blunts card and right now, I couldn't be happier I've never told him.

Fuck him.

I take the room key and my vendor's badge from the clerk. The expo doesn't start until tomorrow morning but the badge gives me access to the conference room tonight if I want to set up.

Thanking the clerk, I turn away from the desk and start to drag my bags toward the elevators.

"Fleur? Oh, it is you!"

I pivot in the direction of the excited voice and am enveloped in a wooly embrace. Mama K, the organizer of Albany's largest fetish festival and ball, hugs me like I'm a long-lost relation. I drown for a moment in her rainbow shawl before I dig my way out and pat her back. She's very huggy for someone I haven't met in person, only on video calls, but it's nice to be welcomed.

"Val!" she calls, a little like a bullhorn so close to my ear. "Come help this doll with her bags."

"Oh, no," I say. "I've got it."

"It's no trouble," she says, holding on to my arm as she steps back from the hug and turns to a young man who puffs over to us. His tight tee-shirt is sticking to his chest and his cheeks are red. It's not at all a bad look on him.

"Take that to Miss Fleur's table," she says, pushing the handle of my huge suitcase at poor Val. "Make sure she has everything she needs."

"Yes, Mama K." Val all but tugs his forelock as he takes my bag and starts wheeling it through the lobby towards a large set of double-doors hung with a banner that reads, "Welcome Children of Lust."

"Now don't worry about setting everything up tonight," Mama K tells me as she pulls me along in Val's wake. "There's plenty of time in the morning. We don't let anyone but vendors in until ten. That gives us all time to have a nice, relaxed breakfast and make sure our tables are—" She smacks a kiss into the air with bright red lips.

"Okay, thank you," I say. "Is it safe to leave samples out on the table over night?"

"Oh, yes. My boys will sleep in the display room to make sure nothing happens. I've never had anything stolen during one of my fests and we're not going to start now, are we?"

"No, ma'am. I just wanted to say again how grateful I am you've let me exhibit—"

She waves my words away. "Nonsense. Your delicious toys will be one of the highlights of the fest. There's no one exhibiting anything like them. I can't wait to hear what people think of them."

I smile nervously. I'm not sure what's worse: exhibiting my toys outside of Blunts for the very first time, or Mama K's expectations. What if no one here likes my scary boys? What if they think they're weird and ugly, the way Nigel does?

For a horrible moment, I want to turn around and go home.

Mama K keeps pulling me forward. Through the double-doors, there's a huge conference room that's already bustling. People surround tables, unloading such a variety of kink equipment that it makes the Blunts marketplace seem tame. There are stands full of dildos. Rainbow displays of floggers. More whips than you'd need to run the Kentucky Derby. Racks of clothes in every variety of leather, lace, feather, vinyl, velvet, and sequin. Oh look, actual racks. A small forest of St. Andrew's Crosses. Spanking benches stacked eight feet high.

I know I'm goggling around like a bumpkin at their first county fair but I can't help it. There are just over a hundred Doms and Dommes at Blunts and about half as many house submissives. With guests, there are often three hundred people in the club on a weekend. By Sunday evening, there's equipment all over the place. And I've still never seen anything like this controlled, kinky pandemonium.

"Here we go," Mama K trills.

She leads me past a table covered with a black cloth, dotted with resin skulls and crystals. A guy behind the table, unboxing a display stand, looks up as we pass. He gives me a smile even more ghoulish than my own: he's in full gray face paint, his eyes sunk in circles of black liner, lips a glossy black. Huge ear plugs stretch his earlobes almost to his shoulders.

I don't have to ask Mama K where my table is to know that the empty one next to Mr. Skulls is mine. The goth corner. That's fine. At least my neighbor won't be upset by what I wear.

Poor Val's dragged my big suitcase behind the empty table. He wipes his face with the sleeve of his shirt and grins at me. "Anything else you need, Miss Fleur?"

"I'm good. Thank you so much."

What am I supposed to do now? Do I offer him a tip the way I would a porter who'd taken my bags to my room? I feel like such a noob.

"Smoke break?" Val says to the goth guy. He nods and leaves the skull and crystal bangles he was draping on the display stand in a pile on the table when he follows Val toward the exit.

"You shout if you need anything at all," Mama K says, blowing air kisses at my cheeks. With a flap of her rainbow shawl, she leaves me at the empty table and disappears into the crowd.

I sag into the chair behind the table. I watch the crowd for several minutes as I try to focus my thoughts. I have a plan for how to set up my table. My friend Brenna helped me design it because she's been to a lot of tattoo expos. I can't remember a thing on it at the moment, but all I have to do is pull it out of my bag.

First I have to call the club and tell someone about the credit card.

Taking several deep breaths, I pull out my phone and call the club. Dan at the desk answers and after telling me neither Master Franco nor Master Cris are available, he puts me through to the Chairman.

Chess picks up immediately. "Everything okay, Fleur?"

"Yes, sir. I've had to use the club credit card. I just wanted you to know I'll pay everything back immediately."

"I know you will," he says, like he's never had any reason to doubt me. "I thought you were in Albany this weekend exhibiting your wonderful creations?"

"I am, sir. Nigel was supposed to come with me but he got stuck at work. There's . . . an issue with his credit card, I guess. The hotel needed another card. But I'll pay cash for the room and any charges that get put on the card, I'll pay them straight back."

Chess hums. "I'm not worried about the card, flower. I'm worried about you. Do you know anyone at the expo?"

"Not really. I've been on some video calls with the organizer and some of the other exhibitors."

"I see. Just a moment." His voice is muffled as he says, "That's a very good girl. Position three and hold for two minutes."

I smile into the phone despite the awkwardness of this conversation. Chairman Chess hooked up with Tessa during the puppy trials last month and has been playing with her ever since.

"If my dear little puppy and I come up tomorrow morning, flower, will you be okay there tonight by yourself?"

My breath catches. "Sir, you don't have to—"

"I know I don't have to. Answer my question."

"Yes, sir. Yes, I'll be okay here tonight by myself and thank you so, so much."

"You're very welcome, flower. Remember, no matter what happens, we are always here for you."

"I know, sir. I just didn't want to ask because this has nothing to do with the club and it's so far away."

"It doesn't matter how far it is, whether you're at the club or out of it. What matters is that your Blunts family is always here for you. I'll text you what time we'll arrive, but we'll plan to be there in time to take you for breakfast. Remind me of which hotel?"

I give him the name, feeling the haze of anxiety lift as he assures me he and Tessa will find a place to stay and look forward to spending the weekend with me in Albany.

"If anything comes up between now and tomorrow morning, call me directly, flower. No hesitating because you think you're imposing. You're not."

"Yes, sir. Thank you, sir."

"Good girl. See you tomorrow."

I say goodbye and put away my phone happily. I never would have asked. And I certainly didn't expect the Chairman to come himself. But I'm so relieved that he is.

Clear and focused, I open my luggage and unpack. After Brenna told her about the expo, Emily made me a beautiful silver velvet table runner. I spread that out carefully, smoothing the few wrinkles from being folded in my bag. Then I set up the collapsible stands I found online and set out my scary boys. A row of demons on the top shelves: Abraxas with his long, curving tongue, Serith with his lapping flange and glow-in-the-dark blues, Zgier's many tentacles, and Azhyyr's gleaming white skull and spined tongue. On the next shelf, my zodiac line: glittering purple Capricorn and onyx Taurus with their double-P horns, blue-green Pisces with its suction cup at the center of each fish, Leo's floppy, crimson mane that's perfect for tickling, the spines and stinger of Scorpio in swirls of red and black. On the bottom shelf, I arrange irritants: molded claws and hooves with their prickling tips, vampire gloves, and carefully labeled lubes in lemon, eucalyptus, pepper, and stinging nettle. Across the open space on the table, I scatter merch with the Midnight Fleur's Monsters logo Brenna's made for me: stickers, keychains, shot glasses.

When I'm finished setting up, I edge the table with strings of fairy lights. I tested them before I left the City but I test them again and smile at the twinkling. I take a picture of the table and pop it into the house submissive group chat.

Brenna: Gonna work more on that logo. Needs to be more phallic.

I grin at my phone. She did a beautiful logo with an outline of Abraxas surrounded by silver lilies on a dark blue background. The open flowers, bulbs, and leaves are already pretty suggestive, but if she can make them even more so, I'm not going to argue with her.

Cappa: Looks great, doll. See you in the morning.

He's coming? Obviously, he is. I don't put the stupid question in the chat because the subbies who are smart, or think they are, like Zuki and Briar, will jump on me. I thumb over to my private chat with Cappa.

You're coming up with the Chairman?

Cappa: With Nigel a no-show? You know it. There's a dozen of us coming. Bed-buddies tomorrow night?

My chin quivers at the support of my Blunts family.

I'd love that.

Cappa: See you tomorrow.

He sends a row of waving hands, clapping hands, and peaches, which make me giggle. Cappa's eighty percent submissive, twenty percent rough, toppy fucker. When he's in his eighties, we're just friends and snuggle buddies. Like most of the house subs when we're not in exclusive relationships.

But when he's in his twenties, damn.

Really hoping he's in his twenties tomorrow. Nigel's been so busy with work that we haven't done a scene in over a month, unless you count his daily morning blowjob as a scene, which I don't when he's too busy to even edge me. I have my usual scenes with Master Javier, Master Theo, Master Cris, and Master Franco every week, and I would never complain about them, but sometimes it's really nice to have the whole night to scene and screw and sleep.

My gothly table-neighbor comes back while I'm texting, smelling strongly of cloves. Ugh, I thought Master Javier's cigarettes were bad.

The goth rummages around in his boxes for a minute and pulls out a feather boa and a handful of glittering strands. "Hey, any chance I could get you to wear some of my stuff tomorrow? You're so pretty, you'll make them look amazing and it'll be a great advertisement."

My cheeks heat. Compliments always feel like touching a gob of phlegm. A wet, nasty shock. But I don't mind helping a fellow artist.

"Sure," I say, holding my hands out.

He drapes the boa over my wrists and coils the chains in my hands. The boa's lovely. Deep black feathers, thick and soft. The necklace is really pretty, too. Three strands of silvery links connecting soft gray crystals and tiny silver skulls. It reminds me of Emily and I've wanted to do something nice for her since she made my table drape.

"How much is the necklace?" I ask.

"Forty-five," Guy Goth says.

I sigh. Since I'm paying for the hotel room on my own now, and with my shifts at Blunts reduced while my ankle recovers, I don't really have forty-five dollars to spare.

"It's beautiful. I'd be happy to wear it and the boa. I brought a bustier, so I'll wear that tomorrow and really show them off." The bustier was part of my outfit for the kinkster's ball tomorrow, but without Nigel, I'm not sure if I should go.

Guy Goth grins, slightly stained teeth flashing between black lips. "Cool."

"I'm Fleur, by the way," I tell him, shifting the necklace over into my left hand and offering him my right.

"Gary," he says, as he shakes.

That makes me smile. Some of the most exotic people have the most mundane names. Except me. My given name really is Fleur. Of course, my mother's given name is Emerald. It's kind of a family tradition.

"Your table looks great," he says. "Any chance you could sprinkle your magic over my table?"

"Sure." I help him rearrange his display until it's more inviting. When we're finished, I take a couple of shots and post them on my social media. A flurry of hearts pop up from the house submissives, followed by hearts and comments from some of the people who have bought my scary boys.

Then one of the comments I dread slides up the screen.

WPAlpha: Where are you, beautiful? Looks like fun.

I swallow and flag the comment. The social media platforms never do anything about them, probably because WPAlpha and the rest of them never say anything outright offensive. Just stalkery shit that makes goosebumps rise, and not in a good way.

WPGamma: See you soon, beautiful.

I flag that one, too, then I put away my phone before their creepy comments ruin my night.

"Thanks for that," Gary says. "So, what are you doing tonight?"

Eating the remaining half of my sandwich and my other donut, watching a movie since the hotel has channels that I won't pay for, and spending quality time with my own personal demon.

"Quiet night," I tell him. "But I'll see you tomorrow."

He smiles sheepishly. "Sure."

Before my rejection makes things weird, I collect the gym bag that has my clothes and toiletries out of my big bag, grab my backpack and handbag, and wave goodbye to Gary.

I pass Val in the hallway, staggering under the weight of a huge box of water bottles. "See you in the bar, Miss Fleur?" he calls to me.

"Not tonight. Thanks for all your help, Val."

"Welcome!" he staggers toward the conference hall door.

In my room, I unpack a little before changing into my swimsuit, a robe, and flip-flops. One of the things that sold Nigel on this expo was the hotel's gym and pool. I guess I'm going to enjoy them on my own.

I feel better after a long kick around the pool on my float. I'm not much of a swimmer, although I've been learning from Brenna's master, who used to be something important in the Navy and is definitely part fish. He was the one who pointed out that I'd recover even faster if I did the physical therapy exercises they gave me for my ankle in the water. He helped me develop a routine and doing it, even in this strange place, settles me. I head back to my room smiling.

After a long shower with the hotel's plentiful hot water, I put a deep conditioner on my hair, plaster an anti-wrinkle mask over my face, pull out my mani-pedi supplies, and dial in to Storytime.

I'm not sure which of the Daddy Doms that Brenna hangs out with now started Storytime, but as soon as she mentioned it, I begged for the link and access code. Master Logan, Master Niall, Daddy Max, Daddy Jack, Daddy Warrin, Miss Ginger, and Daddy Bravo take turns reading for an hour every night. Sometimes they read through one book, night after night. Sometimes they read whatever takes their fancy. Master Niall tends to read poetry and last night I listened to him read T. S. Eliot's "The Wasteland" while silent tears ran down my cheeks. It wasn't just the desolation of the words that moved me. Master Niall has a beautiful voice and with his deep Irish brogue, he could read flat-pack furniture assembly instructions and probably still wring tears out of me.

Not for the first time, I envy Master Niall's two submissives. I'm a sucker for Gaelic accents. Irish; Scottish; English. Drool, drool, drool.

Master Logan uses a lot of British words, but he has a New York accent. It's not the same to my ears.

Tonight, it's Daddy Max's turn. Although he doesn't have an accent, he has a wonderfully deep voice and often adds growls, grumbles, and purrs as sound effects, all of which leave me in a happy, subbie puddle. He's reading a book about a bumblebee who is the policewoman for her hive. Brenna told me it's actually a book Emily's *writing* as a surprise for Cynnie. She's slipping Max a chapter or two whenever she gets them done. Brenna's doing illustrations and they're going to get it printed as Cynnie's Christmas present.

I listen happily to Max's baritone, losing myself in the story, as I take off my old nail polish, file and reshape my nails, and put on fresh, dark gray polish. The story's called the Mystery of the Looted Hive; there are all sorts of suspects that Bramblebee, the hive detective, has to eliminate as she tracks down the hive's stolen honey. Tonight's chapter has Bramblebee facing off with Pepper the Brown Bear, who is definitely my number one suspect. Their banter is hilarious and I giggle so hard I slop nail polish into my cuticles and have to clean it up with a grimace.

Max finishes reading and says goodnight, the way all of them do. "That's all for tonight, my good girls and boys. Night-night, sleep tight, don't let your masters bite . . . too hard."

With a contented sigh, I leave the special chatroom they've set up for Storytime. I flip through the hotel's movies, but nothing strikes me as good aftercare to Storytime. I wait until the quick dry topcoat I've put on my nails is set, wash my face, brush my teeth, braid my hair, pull a black case out of my bag, and climb between the hotel's nice sheets.

I leave a soft light by the bed on so I can see what I'm doing and open the case. Inside is my first scary boy, the prototype for Abraxas. His orange and red colors are muddy because I was still learning how to mix the powders. One of his fangs has broken off because of an air bubble. But I love him.

I've been dreaming about my scary boys since I was little. Finally creating one, using him, finding pleasure with him, freed something in me that I still have trouble talking about. When people ask me why I make my scary boys, I don't have a good answer. I just know that the darkness inside my mind holds more pleasure than fear now.

I squeeze out a little lube and rub it over my scary boy's face. His beak is too pointed, his jaws too wide, and his rippling tongue a little too long. I adjusted the mold after using him for a while. I like all those things about him—his imperfections are perfect for me—but I sell more of the toned-down version.

I trail my personal demon's tongue down over my stomach, leaving a glistening line on my skin and a wet sense of naughtiness. I've done a thousand things dirtier than masturbate, but always with someone else. This is just for me, the ultimate hedonism. A hot thrill at my own deviance pools in my core. The demon's pointed tongue traces the sensation on top of my skin. I circle it around my clit hood and shiver with pleasure.

The touch of the silicone is familiar and yet alien, flexible but firm. Those dichotomies stir me at a deep level. They're what I love about dominance and submission, too. A dance I've done a thousand times, but there's always something different, something unknown, with each scene. The best dominants are steady, solid, and unbending when it comes to their rules, but able to pivot when a scene stops working.

I hook the tongue between my pussy lips and let it sink in slowly. I've used my scary boy so many times, it glides in on muscle memory, without any conscious direction from me. My legs begin to shake as soon as the long tongue pushes against my cervix. It's a completely different sensation from being bumped by a cockhead during deep penetration. This is a much gentler pressure that makes my body blossom. My scary boy's fangs scrape my pussy lips and the sensitive skin around my asshole as he sinks all the way in. The hint of danger fires adrenaline through my blood, even though I know I'm completely safe. My scary boys would never hurt me.

I draw the toy back and fuck myself with it. The undulating base of its tongue rubs against all the best spots. Mini-orgasms fire through me, waves of heat and pleasure that roll up into my belly, building and building toward the big bang. Before I tumble over the edge, I pull my scary boy back and tease my clit and opening with the tip of his tongue. When Nigel has time to scene with me, this is the part he likes best: directing me as I edge myself. I imagine eyes on me, dark and hot and almost angry as they watch me pleasure myself.

I lift my knees and spread for a better angle before I slide my scary boy back inside. I writhe and call out into the quiet room when the undulations catch me just right, when the beak presses perfectly against my most sensitive point, shooting sharp sparks behind my eyes. My legs buck. I pretend a deep, cold voice has ordered me to stillness and tighten the muscles in my thighs to hold position. That makes me clamp down on my scary boy's tongue and shoots me straight over with a scream. The mini-orgasms pool into a hard point deep in my belly. With a shudder, that point fractures into frantic ripples spreading up through my torso, down through my legs. When the ripples hit my heart, I swear it stops for a second. My lungs seize. My feet jerk.

Then all the tension drains out of me in a long gush. Oh, bliss. Oh, peace. I hover in that perfect moment of stillness.

Finally, I let my scary boy slip out of me. I pop him on the built-in bedside table so he can watch over me all night. I curl on my side, pull the sheet and blanket up over my head until I have a cocoon, and close my eyes.

[To be continued . . .]

an impecunious tail – part 2

BLUNTS HOUSE SUBMISSIVES – FLEUR

"HEY, BABE, COME HERE OFTEN?"

I turn into Cappa's brilliant white smile.

I poke his shoulder with my spoon. "You're laying cheesy pick-up lines on me at the breakfast buffet?"

"We can go to the bar instead," he offers. He circles his finger in the air between us. Just that hint of dominance tickles down my spine, raising all the good goosebumps. "Show me."

I twirl, showing off my outfit: beaded black bustier, black tutu edged with midnight blue sequins, shiny black leggings, boots, black feather boa, and Gary's beautiful necklace. I put the bowl I was scooping fruit into down and throw the end of the boa over my shoulder like I'm about to take center stage. "You like?"

"Is your mother a beaver, girl?" When I frown at him, not understanding, he continues, "Cause, dam."

I swat him harder. "Lame! What is wrong with you?"

He raises his hands. Cappa has long, pale fingers with big knuckles. Artist's hands. He's the only guy I've ever wanted to fist me. "It's this place. Budget hotels bring out the cheese in me."

I sigh, wishing this was much more of a budget hotel than its décor suggests. Paying for two nights here is going to leave me really short this month. I only agreed to exhibit at this expo because Nigel said we could turn it into a dirty weekend, and he'd pay for the room.

Nigel didn't even send me a good-morning text. He forgets half the time anyway, but I figured since he left me holding the bag on the hotel room, he'd try to make it up to me a little.

I shake off my dying relationship and focus on someone I know cares about me. Cappa and I have been good friends since he got hired at Blunts, a few months after I did. For a while, I thought we might be more than friends. We hooked up whenever either of us was free. He even lived with me for a couple of months and still has a bunch of his stuff at my place.

But Cappa needs more than I can give him. He has these cycles where he becomes increasingly needy and then goes off the deep end, finding some rando Dom who will really hurt him. He nurses his bruises—and sometimes stitches—while he evens out for a few months. Then he spirals again. All my affection didn't stop the cycles, and I learned a long time ago not to wager my heart on unreliable people.

Cappa seems solid right now. His bruises, and stitches, from his last spiral are mostly healed. He's been spending time with Master Logan and Emily. Master Logan's been topping him—everyone says non-sexually, but knowing what an utter horn-dog Cappa is, I find that hard to believe—and that seems to be keeping him level.

Can I rely on him enough to be more than friends? No. But I can enjoy his twenties and then go my own way, happy that we've made each other happy, if only for a while.

Cappa picks up my bowl and hands it back to me. He shoulders in beside me at the buffet line and loads up his own bowl with cut fruit. Emily may be our resident health food nut, but Cappa's been a healthy eater as long as I've known him. That's why he has a dancer's physique and skin that's even clearer than mine.

Once we make it through the buffet, we join a table that's filling up with my Blunts family. The Chairman and Tessa, Mistress Dana and Austin, Mistress Maude and Hunter, they've all come up to support me. I make a quick circle of the table to give everyone hugs.

I know my eyes are too bright when I look at the Chairman. "Thank you, sir."

"You're welcome, flower. Tell me the agenda for the weekend?"

I take a seat between Cappa and Tessa as I explain the expo schedule with the ball tonight and the closing meal for exhibitors at a local restaurant tomorrow after the two full days of the expo.

Chess nods through it all. "Dana and Austin have to leave tomorrow afternoon for a commitment back in the City. The six of us remaining should all fit in my car, so we'll plan to spend the whole weekend and drive back on Monday morning, not too early. Does that suit you, flower?"

"That would be wonderful, sir."

"Good. Point me at the organizer after you've eaten, and I'll take care of tickets for the ball tonight and a table at dinner tomorrow. Blunts should have been a sponsor of this event. You be sure to tell me about your upcoming exhibitions, flower. I want to make sure the club has a presence at all of them."

The warmth that expands in my chest chases away any of the gloom that Nigel's abandonment cast over this weekend. "I will, sir. Thank you."

"I'll bring it up with Rob and Felix," Mistress Dana says in her clear alto. "We won't miss any more of these."

Chess nods his head. "Thank you, Dana." He taps three fingers against the back of Tessa's hand. She immediately rises, takes his empty coffee cup, and goes to the buffet to refill it.

A shard of longing pricks through my chest at how well-trained Tessa is now. I wish Nigel would develop hand signals like that with me, but he doesn't seem interested.

Cappa leans over and whispers in my ear. "Finish your fruit, then go to the buffet with your hands behind your back, get a cup of water and bring it back to me in your teeth."

I shiver. He's in his twenties.

"Yes, Cappa."

I don't gulp down my fruit. That would only get me frowns from all the Doms at the table. But I eat it a lot faster than I would if I was sitting at the breakfast table alone.

I'm careful with my position when I walk across to the buffet table, crossing my wrists behind me and pushing my shoulders back. My club collar is on display above the glittering strands draped over my upper chest. A lot of eyes touch on the collar and then move away as I perform my task. I'm representing Blunts now, so I want every move to be graceful, perfectly submissive. I use a plastic cup in case something bad happens, gripping the cup's rim tightly between my teeth as I walk back with my hands tucked into the curve above my ass again.

I bow in order to set the cup down on the table beside Cappa's plate. He strokes my bare arm and nods at my seat. "Nice. Sit down, good girl."

Glowing, I sit, lean into him, and whisper, "Thank you, Cappa."

"Happy to top you through the weekend if you want, babe. I'm in the zone."

"I'd love it."

"Great. What tops like a Tiger and blinks?"

"What?"

He blinks rapidly, fluttering his long eyelashes.

I cover my face with my hands and groan. "Is it going to be like this all weekend?"

"Very possibly," he admits. "Are you Jamaican?"

"You know I'm not."

"You sure? 'Cause you're Ja'makin' me crazy."

"If I suck you off before the expo opens, will you stop?"

He grins. "Offer accepted."

He grabs my hand and pulls me to my feet. I wave at everyone as he drags me out of the hotel restaurant.

"Room key," he demands.

I dig it out of my bag and hand it to him, then direct him to the right room. When we go in, he glances around and shakes his head. "You wouldn't even know you stayed here last night."

I shrug. What can I say? When I'm nervous, I clean.

Cappa cups his hand under my chin. "Were you worrying about today?"

I nod.

"No more worrying. Put a pillow down. Get on your knees. Three deep breaths."

I follow his instructions word for word. No one knows like a submissive how to make a blowjob hell or heaven. If I piss Cappa off, he'll make it hell. That's just what he's like as a top. I don't mind blowjob hell occasionally. An uncomfortable blowjob can put me in a good headspace if I've been off and want a reset that makes me feel super subby. But for today, when I'm worried about what the expo will throw at me, I'd rather a blowjob that leaves me relaxed and confident.

I settle onto my knees, tucking my hands beyond me again, the way I know Cappa prefers. He smiles at me as he unzips his jeans and takes out his cock. Cappa's gorgeous head to toe. Like one of those Byronic tragic heroes I've read about: sculpted cheekbones and a killer jaw, a thick, glossy cap of black hair with curls that frame his cheeks and brush his collar, eyes a clearer, brighter blue than even that Irish actor. When he looks at me with those eyes, all I want to do is kneel at his feet, exactly like I am now.

Problem is, most days he wants to kneel, too. I've tried to switch for him. He was nice about it, but I could tell it was a total disappointment for him.

Happily, he doesn't want to kneel today. His eyes have that hard, biting light in them they get when he's deep in topspace. He's not gentle when he slaps his flushed pink cock across my lips. My lips sting and ache when he mashes them against my teeth with his knuckles and cockhead.

I part my lips for him, yielding, wanting him to take my mouth, own my throat.

"Suck. Just the tip."

I carefully engulf him with my lips, filling the front of my mouth with his hot, firm flesh. There's always a moment, when I first take a guy into my mouth, that I'm tempted to bite. I can almost feel it, his skin yielding under my teeth. I can almost hear his gasp as the pain hits. But Cappa doesn't like to be bitten. He'll safe-word out if I bite him now and I don't want to ruin the scene. Maybe, someday, I'll find a guy who wants to be bitten.

It's not today, though.

Hollowing my cheeks, I give him the suction he wants. His pupils dilate, the turquoise of his eyes deepening. His free hand slips into my hair, brushing it back from my temple, balling it into a pinching bunch at the back of my head.

"Lick. Gimme that tongue. Push it up into my slit."

I can barely hold his gaze, I'm trembling, quivering, melting so hard for him. Why can't he be like this all the time? I'd give him anything he wanted; I'd be the perfect sub for him, if only he'd top me all the time.

I cling to that fantasy for a minute as I lave his cockhead with my tongue, alternating broad strokes with flicking licks, curling my tongue to make it as pointed as possible before I press it into the groove of his urethra. I'm rewarded with his deep groans.

"You make it so good for me," he whispers, his voice harsh with pleasure. He squeezes, tugging so hard on my hair that my eyes prickle.

I pulse my tongue against his tip. His cock throbs in my mouth in answer. I'd forgotten how much he loves this sensation. I work it, flicking the point of my tongue against his slit, sucking when I pull my tongue back. Cappa's moans fill the room. The hand gripping my hair shakes.

"Pull back if you don't want me to come in your mouth, babe," he groans.

I refuse to swallow for a lot of the Blunts Doms, mostly to tease them. But I don't mind with Cappa. I suck hard and feel a thrill as hot as his come when he spurts into my mouth.

I gulp it down. As much as I like pleasing my Dom, swallowing does nothing for me. Brenna says she loves it now that she's found her forever-Dom and when he makes her hold it on her tongue before she swallows—fucking gross—she melts into a subbie puddle.

I tease her about Master Mac's magic jizz. But the truth is, I'd kill for someone to make me feel that way.

Cappa releases my hair and strokes it down while he relaxes through the aftermath. "How're you doing, babe? You need me to take the edge off before the expo?"

Stifling my sigh, I shake my head. I don't want him to ask. I want him to tell me I'm not getting any relief before the expo, that he's leaving me on simmer all day, that whether I get a reward tonight will depend on whether I can be a good girl and follow his rules.

Cappa's great in the moment, but it's only for the moment. The rest of the time, he's much too considerate.

"I'm good," I tell him. He helps me to my feet, waits while I fix my hair, and lets me lead him up to the conference room.

"Want me to stay with you at your table today?"

"Yeah, if I show you how to work the app, would you take payments?" I ask.

"Sure."

"I mean, that assumes I sell anything."

Cappa wraps his arm around me. "Make you a bet. If you don't sell out by the end of the expo, I'll give you a dozen foot rubs."

He knows how much I love foot rubs.

"Before Halloween?"

"That's next week."

"I know."

"You drive a hard bargain. Okay, a dozen foot rubs if you don't sell out by the end of tomorrow."

"What's my end?"

"Rim me."

He knows I hate that. "Ugh."

"Deal?" he presses.

"Deal. I hate you."

He chuckles.

I'm grateful for his help, and his humor, when the doors open an hour later and the hall is flooded with people. Who knew there were so many kinksters in Albany? Mama K told me to expect two thousand people. This feels like more than that and all at once.

Cappa's humor helps me cope with the hotel's overloaded internet, which makes the payment app I'm using so slow that I have to give tickets to buyers and ask them to come back to pay later. A pile of numbered boxes grows around my feet and my heart sinks with doubt that people will come back to finish their purchase. I've told them I'll hold their selection until the end of the day, but will that leave me with a pile of unsold stock that I have to lug back home in defeat? The thought makes my stomach curdle.

The morning goes by in such a crazed rush of faces and questions and frustration with the payment app that when Cappa slides a cup of coffee under my nose, I startle. He kisses my cheek before he sits behind the table and dives into a boxed lunch.

Stragglers drift out of the hall as the doors close for an hour. I answer a last question about one of my scary boys for a lady who says she'll come back after lunch before I sit beside Cappa and pick through the box he's brought me. Mama K promised a boxed lunch for all vendors. She's delivered. There's even a little salad in it and the ham and cheese sandwich is on wheat bread, no mayo.

I'm so engrossed in my food, and in getting off my feet for the first time since the doors opened, that I don't even notice the Chairman walk up until he settles a hand on my shoulder.

"That looks grim," he says. "I'm taking everyone to lunch. I appreciate you can't leave your table, but surely we can bring you back something better?"

"Where are you going?" Cappa asks.

The Chairman tells him. Cappa gets out his phone and pulls up the menu—which the hotel wifi works perfectly for, of course—and after a minute of negotiation over carbs, the Chairman pats my shoulder and leaves with our order.

"Sorry you're stuck here with me," I say to Cappa.

He grins. "I'm not. Nowhere I'd rather be, doll face."

"Now, I know that's not true. What's going on with Logan?"

Cappa grimaces. "Brenna's such a snitch."

"I didn't even hear it from her first. Austin and Hunter gossip like little old ladies."

Cappa snorts. "Look, I know it's not going anywhere. Bren already gave me the talk."

"She already gave you the, 'don't try to come between Logan and Emily' talk, or the 'fixating on Logan will prevent you from finding a healthy relationship' talk?"

"Both." Cappa pokes around in his salad with the little wooden fork that the venue's provided with the box lunches. "I wouldn't ever try to come between Logan and Emily."

"I know you wouldn't intentionally. You're not that guy." I reach out and pat his knee. "But you've always had feelings for Logan. A lot of us do. He was the Master of Training for years and it's hard not to have some feelings for the Dom who trained you. If Logan tops you regularly, those feelings will only deepen."

Cappa keeps his eyes fixed on his salad; he nods slowly.

"Either way it ends badly. He reciprocates and you destroy a relationship that's hashtag goals for a lot of us, or he doesn't, and you get your heart broken. Again. Stop before it gets ugly."

"Yeah. I know you're right. I hate to ask but any chance I could stay with you for a little while? I'm about to get evicted."

I rub his knee. "I'd love that. You know you always have a place to crash with me and I could use help with the rent."

His eyes flash up to mine. "Nigel won't mind?"

"Naw, I think Nigel is about done with me anyway. This weekend." I shrug. "Whatever. I'll just put the stuff he's left at my place in a box and leave it at his office reception. That'll be clear enough."

As clear as him canceling the credit card for the hotel room.

Cappa scoots his chair a little closer to mine and slides his arm around my shoulders. "Sorry, babe. I didn't even ask what went wrong."

"The usual. I'm too needy. He's too erratic. I won't give up the club. He's married to his job. He wants a fifties housewife outside the bedroom. I want a fucking adult who does his own dishes and puts in a load of laundry when he sees the hamper's full. Whatever. I'm the only one of us trying to make it work . . . and you know that never does."

"No, it doesn't." He gives a sad, little laugh. "Bren made me pinkie swear that we'd both stop looking for Doms in all the wrong places. She found her forever-Dom like two seconds later."

"We're not that lucky," I commiserate. "But if you take a step back from Logan, I'll take a step back from Nigel and we'll both look for better Doms."

He lifts his free hand, holding out his pinkie. I curl my pinkie around his and shake.

"I know the first place I'm looking," he tells me as we go back to our salads.

"You already found someone?"

"Let's say, he has potential. And I definitely need to grab him before he finds some Little to dote on."

I wrinkle my nose. "He's a Daddy-Dom?"

"Don't make that face. Logan is, too."

"Logan was a regular Dom first. And a sadist. I still don't understand how that works with him and Emily—"

Cappa grunts. "Trust me, it works."

"You'd know, but I still think it's weird. Daddy-Doms are all soft and cuddly—"

"You don't know anything about Daddy-Doms, doll face. None of us really do because there haven't been any at the club. Trust me,

Logan is not soft and cuddly with Emily. At least, not most of the time. He's stern and strict, but loving, too. Like . . . a good father. Anyway, I think this guy is going to be at the Halloween party Emily's organizing. I'll introduce you."

"That's the day before Halloween, right?" I ask. I have plans with some vanilla friends, but I'll break them if Cappa really wants me to meet this Dom.

"Yeah, you free? You're not working that night, are you?"

"No, I'm off. I haven't been invited, though."

"It's open to anyone in the club but I'll make sure you get an invite. Don't worry."

"Thanks."

We finish up our salads a few minutes before the doors reopen. I spend a minute restocking the table and rearranging the piles of boxes at my feet so I don't constantly trip over them. A glance around the hall shows a lot of the vendors aren't at their tables. I guess they decided they needed something more than ham and cheese on wheat and a salad.

"Hey, would you mind standing at that table and just keeping watch over his stuff until he gets back?" I ask Cappa when I see that Gary-the-Goth isn't back yet.

"Sure." Cappa moves the few steps over just as the doors open.

The hall floods with people again. The lady asking questions about Serith makes a beeline back to my table. She has a few more questions but what she really wants becomes clear when she asks if I could do Serith in custom colors. I pull out the body-safe powder color chart I have from the manufacturer I buy from and within a few minutes, she's picked the colors and given me a deposit on a custom order, thankfully in cash.

Maybe half of the people who reserved one of my toys come back in the afternoon as the hotel's wifi struggles on. Seeing the pile of boxes decrease lifts my spirits, as does the spicy calamari and cheesecake that the Chairman brings back from their lunch. Tessa spells me while I eat; Austin gives me one of his amazing neck rubs, and I launch back into the sea of faces and questions with a real smile instead of a forced one.

At some point, Cappa returns to stand beside me and takes over the battle with the wifi. When I look over, I see that Gary's returned to his table. He gives me a little wave and mouths "thank you" while displaying one of his bracelets for a potential buyer.

The hall doors close at five so everyone has time for dinner before getting ready for the ball. I do a quick stock take and realize that I've sold way over half of what I brought, and I've got a dozen custom orders. That makes paying for the hotel room much less of a problem and even unboxing the toys that people reserved but never came back for doesn't sour my mood.

Gary-the-Goth's talking with Cappa when I finish. Well, Gary's talking and Cappa's flirting, but that's just Cappa. When I move over beside them, Cappa wraps his free arm around me, but doesn't stop touching Gary's veiny forearm.

From their conversation, I pick up that Gary went with Mama K, Val, and a bunch of other vendors to a nearby restaurant for lunch. On the way back, there was a three-car accident on the road between the restaurant and the hotel. The traffic rolled back so badly that they got out of their cars and taxis and walked the mile and a half to the hotel, which is why they were all so late.

When Cappa takes a breath, Gary reaches out and touches the necklace I'm wearing.

"Looks like it was made for you. Keep it. Small thank you for having Cappa watch my stuff. Some people had things walk off while their booths weren't staffed."

"That's such a shame," I say. "Mama K told me nothing's been stolen during her expos."

"Yeah, her unblemished record's got a big stain on it now. Val was saying they're still adding it up, but it looks like about a grand's worth."

I wince. That's a big deal. The kink community is pretty small, and word will get around about something like that.

"Mama K's facing off with the hotel. She says they shouldn't have opened the doors with so many vendors away from their tables," Gary continues.

I shrug. People always point fingers when something like this happens, but there's no way the hotel is going to pay for what's been lost. The best they can hope for is an insurance pay-out, and that will take months.

"Anyway, I appreciate you two looking out for me," Gary says. "I'll see you at the ball later, right?"

"Wouldn't miss it," Cappa responds with a wink. "Let's go get ready, huh, doll face? Takes time to achieve this degree of perfection."

He tosses his head, swishing his glossy mane. Gary and I laugh at him.

The Chairman and Tessa catch up to Cappa and me as we're leaving the exhibition hall.

"Flower, I know you've been rehabbing your ankle in the pool. Could I tempt you to swim with me and my puppy?" The Chairman asks.

I nod eagerly.

"Excellent. We'll meet you in the pool in fifteen minutes, unless you need longer?"

"No, sir. I'll be there in fifteen."

The Chairman nods and leads Tessa away by the lead clipped to her thick, spiked collar.

"I didn't bring a suit," Cappa grumbles.

"I brought two. You can borrow one of mine."

"I know you're teasing, but I will take you up on that."

"I wasn't teasing. One of my suits is a two piece with boy shorts. You'll be fine in the shorts."

Cappa grins and goodness, that is a heart-stopping grin. "Not that I'm insecure in my masculinity, but that's a relief."

"Come on, you'd rock my one-piece."

"I would," he agrees. "But I'm not speedo-ready."

I laugh at him. Some of the male house subs wax themselves as bare as I do, but not Cappa.

"Nothing wrong with showing a little bush," I say, tweaking the crotch of his jeans. "It's all natural."

He sniggers. "Tell Master Ten that. I manscape just to avoid him taking clippers to me."

We giggle our way back to the room.

***

"Ride it, babe," Cappa tells me, pushing me forward onto my scary boy's long tongue. He pumps deep in my ass as I impale myself over and over on my demon, stuck to the bathroom door with a suction cup. I cling to the door with one hand and Cappa's neck with the other as spikes of heat shiver through me.

Cappa nudges my feet a little wider, pushing his knees between mine as he fucks up into me. What feels like way too many inches pulling out and driving in again. My eyes roll back at the depth of the double-penetration. "Fuck, Cap, fuck, fuck."

"Take it, slut," he growls at me. His hand snakes around my bare chest and collars my throat. "You breathe when I say you do. You come when I say you do."

I sag against the door, every muscle melting at his dominance. "Yes, Cappa."

He lets me rest my forehead against the door but pulls my ass back so he can pound me even harder. Good thing I don't have much chance to sit down while I'm exhibiting because I'm going to be sore tomorrow. He's not usually this vigorous. I guess rubbing up on each other during the swim and dinner was a turn on.

He closes off my throat until my head spins. We've both been choked enough to know exactly how to do it. He controls the flow of blood into my head, but never shuts off my airway. I pant raggedly and watch the room loop in beige and white circles around us as hot, bright tingles spread all through me.

He pulls out of my ass suddenly and smacks it.

"New position," he tells me. "Bend over backwards."

"Bu-backwards?"

For a dazed moment, I'm not sure what he means. Then it tracks, but I have no idea how to get from the position I'm in to the position he wants.

He pulls me off my demon's long tongue, spins me around, and shoves me to my knees. Then he slaps me across the face with his wet cock.

I collapse to the floor. No Dom's ever hit me with the cock that's just been in my ass. I'm not sure if it's too much or if this is just Cappa at the dommiest anyone's ever been with me. I blink at him, unable to even process for a moment.

Cappa grabs me by the hair and pulls my head back. "Are you safe wording?"

Am I? I don't know. I'm still reeling from the fucking and the oxygen deprivation and the cock-slap. My pussy and ass are clench-ing. My body's throbbing. Maybe it was a little too much, but I don't think I'm calling red.

Instead, I sag onto my back, get my feet and hands under me, and push up into a handstand. Cappa doesn't let go of my hair until I'm in a full backbend and I'm not sure if the tears in my eyes are from the pain of his grip or being overwhelmed.

With a rip, Cappa opens a condom package and rolls it on. Then he grabs my left leg, wraps it around his waist, and shoves into my pussy.

"Fuck!" My weight shifts completely onto my arms as he pushes into me. I throw my head back for balance. There's a see-saw moment where I'm sure we're going over, then Cappa pulls back on my thigh and I find my center. I firm up my stance as he starts pumping.

I can't possibly come like this, balancing on my hands and one foot. But with my back arched and my belly-button pushing toward the ceiling every time Cappa pistons into me, each thrust hits some very good spots.

"Jesus, fuck!" A noise between a bark and a moan breaks out of me.

"Fucking take it," Cappa growls, pumping furiously.

A wave of sensation ripples through me and for a moment I'm not sure if it's pain or pleasure. Then every muscle locks. Cappa howls wordlessly. My body clamps down on his and explodes. Everything spins. The room. My head. My belly. I ride along the edge of pleasure and pain, too much and exactly enough.

Cappa pinches my clit and I explode again. This time it is too much. I shriek and whimper as my body bucks. I can't even fight against him in this position. All I can do is hold it so we don't fall and suffer through the waves of sensation. The white-hot light of my orgasm goes over to an electric shock running through my blood, burning and fizzing. Cappa grabs me around the hips and waist, holding me up as he finishes, groaning and jerking inside me. Then he lets me slide to the floor.

He stands over me, his jeans around his ankles, hands on his hips, head thrown back.

I manage to lift my foot and poke his thigh with my toe. "You are fucking crazy."

"C'mon, admit it, that was good."

"That was deranged, and I think I pulled my hammy."

Cappa chuckles and sags to the floor. He pulls my feet across his thighs and begins lazily working his thumbs up and down my hamstrings.

"Better?"

"You're still nuts. Did you actually hit me in the face with your dick when it's been up my ass? That's so unsanitary."

"Hey, I did it right. I hit the flat of your cheek. Nowhere near your eye or mouth. Besides, you scene with Master Ten every week. I know you clean yourself out for him."

"I do, but, fuck, Cap. I honestly would have been shouting red if it was anyone but you."

He tips his head back against the edge of the bed and chuckles. "Good thing it was me. You've never done the bridge before? You looked so fucking surprised."

"No, I've never done it before, you crazy person. I wasn't even sure I could do it. And if you hadn't pulled my leg around your waist, I'm pretty sure I would have broken my neck as I overbalanced."

He lifts my leg into the air, stretching my hamstring. I grimace at him, even as the tendon loosens.

"I had you. I know it's been a while, but we've danced together before. I've never dropped a partner. I wouldn't have let you fall."

"You're still crazy," I tell him.

"Yeah, I know. I'm too much." He goes quiet and I realize he's not talking about his choice of sexual positions.

"Cappa." I sigh. "Someday you're going to find your Goldilocks Dom and you're going to be just right."

"Both of us, huh?" He pats my leg. "Someday. C'mon, let's shower. We've only got an hour before the ball starts."

I groan but climb up off the floor and help him up. After the intense sex, our shower is almost platonic, with just a little kissing and washing each other's hard-to-reach places. Like an old, married couple. Except that Cappa and I aren't meant to be together.

Sometimes, it feels like God or Fate or just my own brain chemistry is having a big laugh at my expense.

Cappa demands a mini fashion show, so I show him the four outfits I brought. He rejects the long skirt I'd planned to wear. Instead, he has me put a black slip under my corset and pin up the thigh-length skirt so my suspenders and the tops of my stockings show.

"Show off those gorgeous legs, babe," he tells me.

I put Gary-the-Goth's necklace back on and flirt at myself in the bathroom mirror with his feathered boa. Feeling beautiful, I do a light face of makeup since my skin's good right now. I go heavy on the eyeliner and when he doesn't object, line Cappa's eyes, too. It's not fair how much some black liner makes his every glance smolder.

I punch him playfully. "You're too hot for your own good."

He rolls his shoulder and strikes a pose. "I know it, darling."

"Idiot."

"Baby cakes."

"Ass."

"You're gonna have to eat mine this time tomorrow. I bet you sell out by lunchtime."

I scowl at him in the bathroom mirror where I'm primping. "Mama K said Saturday's the busier day."

He gathers up my hair and begins running my brush through the ends. "Keep hoping, babes. You're going to have that tongue up my ass before you know it."

I stick it out at him in the mirror.

He laughs.

Walking into the ball on Cappa's arm is a thrill, I won't lie. Even though we're not *together*, it's still kind of awesome to be with the prettiest guy in the room. Which is not to say that Cappa is effeminate, although he's very in touch with his feminine side. So in touch that he wears a deep blue, crushed velvet pirate shirt, open to his waist, over his black leather pants, without a flicker of self-consciousness.

He knows he looks good in anything he wears and he's not dressing to impress. He's just Cappa.

The ballroom's set up with a bar at one end and the dance floor at the other. Someone's made an attempt at decorating the room. Black and gold cloth is draped in fans around the light fixtures; ice sculptures in the shapes of paddles are gently melting at each end of the bar. But the real decorations are the people. Cappa's outfit is conservative and even mine is tame in comparison to what others are wearing. There's a man being led around by piercings through his nose, lip, nipples, and foreskin, golden chains running from under a short toga. One woman's dancing in a pair of thigh-high boots and a few strips of latex across her full breasts and hips. No one's complaining about how much skin she's showing.

Cappa observes that her beauty would be enhanced with a butt plug as we pass her onto the dance floor. I elbow him and thank my lucky stars he didn't think of "enhancing" my outfit that way. Dancing with a butt plug in is a serious challenge.

After a dance, I leave Cappa to circulate. You never know where you'll find your forever-Dom and I don't want to cramp his style. The Chairman claims a slow dance and asks me about how the day went. He's always been amazingly supportive of my side hustle. As soon as I was ready to sell my scary boys, he had me exhibit them at the club. My first customers came through Blunts and I'm sure he was behind the enthusiastic reviews those customers posted on my website.

When the song ends, Austin asks for a dance. He whirls me around the crowded dance floor. I've heard several people mention how small the conference room where the ball's being held is this year. It is crowded, but I like it. It feels intimate instead of intimidating. Blunts feels that way to me, too.

I look up into Austin's deep brown eyes. His smile flashes.

"Happy?" I ask him.

"Yeah, of course. Nice to get away from the City for the weekend."

"I meant with Dana. You happy?"

His smile spreads into his eyes and lights them, glossy and warm. "I guess."

He's not fooling anyone.

I tug on his two collars: the plain leather club collar and a metal collar with a tag on it that looks like a dog tag. There's nothing printed on the side facing me. I know *Property of Dana* is etched on the side touching his skin. "Has it worked out with the club?"

"Yeah, DirtyGurl paved the way. No issue with me being exclusive with my Mistress. I'm still on the desk four days a week and medical backup."

"I'm happy for you, Austin. You deserve it."

He hugs me without breaking the rhythm of our steps. "We all deserve it."

At some level I believe that. Master Javier's been telling me for years that I deserve to be loved. But at another level, the girl whose family sold her virginity at thirteen and pimped her out for years still wonders.

I make a mental note to bring that up at our next group therapy session and then push it out of my mind so I can enjoy the night.

It's after two in the morning, the ice sculptures have completely melted, and my whole body's sore, when Cappa drags me away from the Chairman, who is still leading me around the nearly empty dance floor.

"You're going to be so sorry in the morning," he tells me.

I grin at him. I don't care. Nights like this, with my Blunts family, are to be cherished.

"We need more balls at the club," I say as we weave our way back to my room with our arms around each other.

"I agree with that. Bet if we put a suggestion in to Master Logan, he'd make it happen."

I don't argue with him, because something like that, Master Logan probably would make happen. But Cappa's renewed faith in the Dom who trained us and left us to fend for ourselves makes my heart hurt.

"Cap, I'm not going to give you the talk again, but please, please don't put your faith in Master Logan too soon."

"I'm not," he says quickly. Then, more slowly, he adds. "I believe he's going to try to make things better."

"I believe he has good intentions. Master Logan's not an uncaring man. But he'll put Emily first. Just wait until she has a crisis. That'll be the last we see of him for a while. Just like when Master Ryan's wife had complications with her pregnancy. The masters who have collared submissives always put them first. I don't blame them. It's just a fact."

"You're right," Cappa admits, opening the door to my room with the key card. "I need some space from him. Thanks for letting me move back in with you."

I hug him before I kick off my boots and strip off. I'm not self-conscious around Cappa, but I dive into the shower for a quick clean up. He doesn't need to smell my sweaty stink.

He bombs in and out of the water with me, wraps himself around me while I brush my teeth and moisturize, then picks me up and carries me to the bed. He's inside me before he even lays me down on the bed. When he pushes me up the bed into the pillows I follow his lead, but when it seems like he's going to make love to me in missionary, I push at his shoulders and roll us over.

There might be a day when I let Cappa make love to me, but it's not going to be today. I need him to top me, preferably roughly, so my stupid feelings don't get all tangled again. I ride him and as we both get close, I dismount, turn around, and mount him again in reverse cowgirl.

Unlike the craziness he had me doing earlier, this is our favorite position. Tried, tested, and true. It has him howling and bucking up into me in a few minutes. And I can always count on him to get his thumb into my ass, so I come shaking and swearing as I grip his knees and twerk until he sees stars.

After we've cleaned up, he spoons around me. "Missed you," he whispers into my hair.

I pat his arm around my waist and close my eyes without answering him.

The second day of the expo is a million times easier than the first.

I take my prescription painkillers as soon as I get up so I'm not distracted by the soreness of my feet, and legs, and ass. There are fewer vendors exhibiting the second day and that lightens the load on the hotel wifi enough that payments finally go through on the first try. Mama K was right that Sunday isn't as busy, and I have time to talk with everyone who comes to my table. I danced with anyone who asked me last night—although with so many from my Blunts family there, I never had a shortage of partners—and lots of my dance partners come by my table to reminisce about how much fun we had.

With Chairman Chess's blessing, I put a stack of Blunts nightclub passes on the table. They disappear only a little faster than my toys. I don't quite sell out by lunch, but my stock's so low that I accept the Chairman's invitation to lunch at a nice restaurant about twenty minutes from the venue and sell my last scary boy less than an hour after we return.

Cappa slings his arm around my shoulders as we watch the customer walk away, holding the brown bag with my logo printed on the side open and chattering to her friend as they peer inside at Abraxas. Who stares back at them.

"So, about that rim job."

I lean my head on his shoulder. I've made enough this weekend that paying for the hotel doesn't hurt, I'm not worried about the rent, and next month is looking bright instead of anxiety-inducing. "Whenever you want."

His shoulder jerks. "Changed your tune."

"It's been a good weekend."

He kisses my temple. "Yeah, it has, babe. You're not getting out of it, though."

"I'm not trying to. I'm up for it tonight."

After we go out for dinner. And I eat something really, really spicy.

[The end . . . for now.]

a rambunctious tail

MASTER LOGAN, DADDY MAX, EMILY, AND CYNNIE - LOGAN

"WHERE'S MY LITTLE VICTIM?" I call as I stroll into the Blue Harem room.

Two heads pop up from the mounds of pillows covering the room's round, veil-draped bed.

"Victim and victim's guest," Emily chirps.

"Victim's guest? Who is this unsanctioned interloper in my scene?"

"Me, me!" Cynnie, Max's adorable little, wearing a black-and-yellow striped romper and kicking her feet up behind her as she lies on her stomach, waves her hand over her head.

"You, you? What are you, you doing in my scene, bumble-girl?"

Cynnie giggles. "Emmy invited us. She says you're going to show Oppa how to spank me properly."

"I see. And did you think about asking me before making this unsanctioned swerve to my plans, baby doll?"

Now it's Emmy who giggles like the utter mischief she is. "I did, Daddy. Check your WhatsUp."

"My what?"

"The app I showed you over the weekend, remember? The one that doesn't cost anything?"

I scratch the back of my neck. She did show me something over the weekend, but it seemed complicated and I was more interested in giving her a bath and a hard fucking than understanding yet another app when I already have a hundred I don't use.

"I may need you to show me again, little girl," I admit.

She grins. "Did you not check WhatsUp today?"

"Eh, no."

"You have lots of messages, Daddy."

"Great. Give me a summary."

"Max and Cynnie are coming over for lunch." She ticks the points off on her fingers. "Bren's taking Cynnie and me to the club to swim. Cynnie and Max are going to join us for our scene and dinner. I love my daddy."

I hook my hands around the support posts of the bed and lean over the two submissives, who grin up at me, half buried in piles of pillows. "I like that last one, little girl."

"I sent it to you five separate times."

"Five times! And I didn't respond to a single one?" I slap my hand to my forehead. "What am I like, little girl?"

"You didn't even leave me on read, Daddy. Just delivered."

"Atrocious. Egregious. How do you put up with me?"

Emily wriggles happily. "I endure it for the snuggles."

I lean down and kiss the tip of her nose. "This luddite loves you."

"I think you're more of a technophobe than a luddite, Daddy."

"I really hate all these snaps and apps."

Giggles out of the two girls, which is what I was aiming for.

"Where is Max?" I ask.

"Oppa went to ask if Kells could make the rabbit dish with chicken instead of bunny," Cynnie says earnestly.

"Kells should always substitute chicken for bunny," Emily rejoins.

"Technically, it's not bunny," I say, fearing for the menu at the Trattoria. If rabbit is off the menu, my osso buco might be next.

"I don't want to eat Peter Rabbit, Daddy Logan," Cynnie says, blinking up at me with huge, innocent eyes.

"Or Flopsy, Mopsy, and Cottontail," Emily says.

"Er, no, of course not."

"We can't keep rescue bunnies in the Stables with Harry the Mini-Goat and have bunny on the menu down the hall, Daddy," Emily tells me. "It's hypocritical."

I hear the distant death knell of my osso buco. "Uh, I see."

I'm saved from any discussion about the ethics of eating veal by Max's arrival. He strolls in, gives me a chin lift, and jumps onto the bed, pouncing on his little and caging her in with his arms and legs.

"Oppa's rabbit rescue mission was a success, my bumble baby," he tells her, nuzzling into her neck. "Chicken ragu with tagliatelle will be served at eight."

She squeals and throws her arms around her daddy. "Thank you, Oppa."

I wait for them to finish their cuddle and for Max to look up before I rib him. "Finally decided to learn how the pros do it, huh?"

Max scoffs. "You take the hand. You apply the hand to the bottom. Rinse. Repeat. Not all that challenging. Emmy wanted company."

"Amateur," I tell him. "Emmy, how many kinds of spankings are there?"

"Mmm, two."

"Only two?"

She nods sagely, her curls a dark froth against the satin pillows. "The kind where I'm allowed to come and the kind where I'm not allowed to come."

Cynnie giggles.

I tap the tip of Emily's nose with my finger. "Is that all that matters, little girl?"

"Pretty much, Daddy."

"Good news for you, then, since you're allowed to come tonight."

"Wee!"

I chuckle at her adorable enthusiasm and give her an upside-down kiss.

"Spiderman Daddy," Cynnie breathes when I pull back.

Emily wiggles wildly among the pillows.

"Shall we start with an over-the-clothes spanking, little girl?"

"Boooring," Emily and Cynnie chorus.

"I see. Dissention in the ranks already. But in the interests of showing Max the proper way to do a spanking, I think it's important we start with over-the-clothes."

Emily pouts, her soft, jutting lip looking too kissable to resist. I don't even try, kissing her thoroughly and giving her a nip before I release her mouth, which sets her off giggling again.

"Up you get, monkey. It'll be easiest for Max to see what we're doing if we use the bench." I hold out my hand.

"Okay, Daddy." Emily rolls out of the bed. When she stands, I realize what she's wearing.

It's a clown suit.

It's a cute clown suit, with soft blue flannel bottoms held up with rainbow suspenders over a black-and-white Harlequin bodysuit. Bright red socks. No face paint and, thank God, no white contacts. But still . . .

Clown.

After Halloween, she knows how I feel about clowns.

"Baby, what are you wearing?"

She loops her thumbs under her suspenders and runs them up and down. "Like it, Daddy? I'm Spanko the Clown."

I swallow. I hate it.

"I'm not overly keen on clowns, baby."

She grins. "I got that sense at Halloween, Daddy."

"Then you're just being naughty, winding Daddy up."

"I'm not breaking any rules," she points out.

"No, but this is right on the edge of bratting," I answer, feeling an itch in my palms.

Holding out her suspenders, she twists from side to side. "Is it?"

She knows it is.

"I see how it is, little girl. I've promised you orgasms and I won't go back on my word, but you might wish you'd gotten the other kind of spanking."

Her eyes widen. "Eep."

"Uh-huh. You know what you've been angling for. Now you're going to get it. Up on the bench, naughty baby."

She shimmies over to the two-tiered, padded bench. She settles her forearms on the higher piece of the bench, slots her shins into the lower piece of the bench, and sticks out her ass.

Really angling for it.

I glance back at the bed and find that Max has Cynnie over his knee. There's a trap door in her bumble-bee romper, which will come in handy later, but for now it's buttoned up. Both Cynnie's romper and Emily's horrible clown pants have pockets in them, so this is going to be a soft spanking to start. That won't make my little masochist happy.

I position myself beside the spanking bench and run my hand down Emily's sweetly curved back. She gives me a happy murmur.

"You can use over-the-clothes as a warmup," I tell Max. "Instead of warming up the skin by rubbing it with your palm. It's still better to start easy to minimize bruising. But some little girls like marks as a reminder."

"Me, Daddy!" Emily chirps.

"Yes, you, monkey." I give her bottom a pat, then bring my hand down square on the pocket of her clown pants.

Glitter explodes all around me. A hurricane of pink and gold. A fucking plastic tornado. I sneeze, but that only creates an eddy in the shower of sparkling particles. I bat it away from my face. Which only makes it worse. My flailing stirs up a fresh snowfall of the damn stuff.

"What the fuck?"

I blow and wave and get enough of the crap away from my face that I can see Max, who is sitting in the middle of his own cloud of glitter.

As the sparkly shower settles in drifts over everything, I hear tandem giggling.

"Emily," I growl.

"Yes, Daddy?"

"Does this explosion of craft herpes have anything to do with you?"

"Seems to have more to do with *you*, Daddy."

"Since I'm confident neither Max nor I had a packet of glitter up our sleeves, I find that hard to believe."

"Are you sure, Daddy?"

"Very sure, little girl." I pause while Max sneezes hard enough to blow down a brick wall. "Do the clown pants come with a glitter bomb?"

"They didn't *come* with a glitter bomb, no," she says, tipping her head to the side.

"Did they *acquire* a glitter bomb at some point between the time you bought them and today?"

She sniggers. "They might have, Daddy."

"I see." I look over at Max, sitting in his own pile of glitter and tiny, plastic bees. "Mind if we change up the scene?"

He spits glitter off his lip and clamps his hand in his submissive's silky mop of hair, which is shaking with her silent laughter. "What'd you have in mind?"

"I think we relocate to the Stocks and hunt down two little girls who need to be taught a lesson. I'll show you the correct method for applying wooden rulers to bottoms."

"Eek," says Emily.

Max grins. "I'm up for that."

I smack Emily on the ass-cheek without a pocket, sending up a small puff of glitter. "Up, you menace. Go find a Dustbuster."

Emily slides off the spanking bench, twisting her hands together in front of her. "Am I in trouble?"

"You know you are."

"It's National Glitter Day," she protests. "We're celebrating!"

Cynnie climbs off her daddy's lap and stands next to Emily, nodding her head. "Pooyah, glitter."

"If it was National Elephants Day and you brought a parade of elephants to my club, I wouldn't be best pleased with you either. Get a Dustbuster. Let's get this crap cleaned up and then you will face the consequences."

Chastened, both littles hang their heads as they shuffle toward the dungeon door.

I'm tempted to lighten the mood until I hear Emily whisper to Cynnie, "Pooyah, Littles' Army."

[The Littles' Army will return.]

a circuitous tail

MASTER JAVIER AND FLEUR – FLEUR

WHY IS it that the wrong guy always shows up with flowers?

The guy with the flowers, who rises from the bench in the small entryway to my apartment building as I walk in, is not the guy I want to see.

I'd take literally *any* of the other Doms in my life. There are nearly a hundred to choose from. There's also the part-time one who has taken the train two more stops to pick up stuff from his apartment before coming back to mine. I'd even take Master Karl, although he'd be more likely to show up with a flogger than flowers.

"Babe," the wrong-Dom begins.

I stop and put my bag and keys down on my big rolling case. My arms are aching from the set up and take down and hand-shaking and the crazy positions Cappa had me hold. He really is a demon when he's in his twenties.

The ache in my arms is a reminder of how much Nigel wasn't there this weekend. Not to help me carry and set up and take down. Not to make me hold crazy positions. Not to do anything, when he promised he'd be at my side this weekend because he knew how much I was juggling.

"Hi, Nigel," I say.

"Let me take that for you, babe. You take these." He holds out the flowers in one hand and his free hand for my bag.

I stare at him for a long moment. He wasn't there for me this weekend. He didn't even send a good morning text. Cappa's not a full-time Dom and he gave me a hundred times more than Nigel has in weeks.

At the end of the day, the only person you answer to, is you.

I take a deep breath and as I exhale, I shake my head. "No thank you, Nigel."

His handsome face falls. "Babe, I know I let you down. Let me make it up to you. Let's talk and then I'll take you out to dinner. You can tell me all about your thing—"

"My thing that paid for the room when you canceled your credit card?" I say and wince at how sharp my own voice sounds. I don't want to be a bitch. I really don't. And I hate arguing about money. But him leaving me hanging stung.

"Now, just slow down. I ended up on the hook for the clients' dinner and drinks on Friday. My card was maxed. I didn't want you to go through the embarrassment of having the card declined when you went to check out. I made sure they'd let you pay cash before I canceled it."

I shake my head at him. "What if I didn't have enough cash?"

His Adam's apple works in his strong, corded throat. Nigel's gorgeous. Dark, wavy hair. Dark eyes. Seasonless tan. Swimmer's build.

I've been fooled by outward beauty before, but Nigel said and did all the right things when we first met. I thought his internal darkness matched mine. He fed on my pain and I reveled in giving it to him. But he hasn't made time for me in weeks and it probably makes me a needy bitch, but I need more than a Dom's occasional attention.

That's why I went looking outside of Blunts for a Dom in the first place.

This weekend made me realize how much more I could be getting.

"I would have wired you cash," Nigel says, holding out the flowers again. "All you had to do was call. I'd never leave you like that."

But he did.

"Hey." He steps closer and strokes his fingertips down the side of my face. "You didn't call me once all weekend. I figured you were busy, so I didn't bother you, but you know I'm here for you. I wouldn't have left you in the lurch if you needed me."

My throat tightens. He's saying all the right things again. And I'm the bitch who didn't call, didn't text, spent the weekend fucking another guy. Nigel's always been very accepting of my job at Blunts. He knows I have sex with the Blunts Doms. But we don't have an open relationship. Nigel's always said I'm enough for him; he's exclusive with me.

And Cappa's not exactly a Blunts Dom.

Nigel draws me into his chest and hugs me with one arm, keeping the flowers to the side so we don't crush them between us. They're beautiful. Purple and blue and sprigs of gold. The colors Nigel knows I love.

"Come on, babe. I know you're upset. Let me make it up to you. Nice dinner. I don't need to work tonight. We'll scene." He dips his head and rubs his nose along mine. "I know you've been a naughty girl while we've been apart. You can show me all the ways you were bad and I'll show you what happens to bad girls."

He has no idea all the ways I've been bad. And I couldn't show him right now because there's no way I could hold that bridge position with how sore my arms and shoulders are.

But his offer also throws cold water over the warm fuzzies I'm getting from his grovel. Cappa's bringing dinner along with his stuff.

And if he's still in his twenties, I'd much rather scene with him. With the person who dropped everything to support me when he heard I was struggling, rather than the person who caused me to struggle in the first place. Even if Cappa's in his eighties, I'll happily just cuddle with him.

I step back, shaking my head. "I'm sorry, Nigel. I can't. I've made plans."

"For tonight? Babe, break them." He picks up my bag. "You know I don't get many nights free. You know I'm working so hard so I can move up the ladder and give you everything you deserve. I know you're feeling neglected. I'm trying to make it up to you."

Throat tight, I shake my head and look away from his pleading eyes. "I can't—"

My phone pings.

Grateful for the diversion, I pull it out of my jeans pocket.

Cappa: Master Logan wants me to stay here tonight to talk about what's going on at Blunts. You don't mind if I come tomorrow, do you? If you do, TELL ME.

The lump in my throat swells. This is why we're just friends with benefits. Because I can't count on Cappa, either.

Me: All good. See you tomorrow.

Nigel brushes my cheek. "That was your plans canceling wasn't it? I can tell by your face, babe. Come on. Let's take your stuff upstairs. You can freshen up. Put your wig and a pretty dress on. I'll take you to Elton's. You love Elton's."

I do love Elton's. I can't afford Elton's, though, and I wonder how Nigel can if his credit card is maxed.

At the end of the day, the only person you answer to, is you.

There have been many times that I've gone to bed with someone I knew would let me down in the morning just so I didn't have to go to bed alone. Maybe I'm getting old or maybe I've just had enough disappointment.

I'd rather go to bed alone tonight.

"I'm sorry, Nigel, no." I square my shoulders and pull my bag out of his hand. "You did let me down. In a big way. This isn't something you can make up to me with a dinner and a scene. Not after neglecting me for weeks. I've had a long day; I want to shower and get into my pajamas and have a glass of wine. I'll call you."

I grab the handle on my rolling bag and pull it after me as I walk to the elevator, thankful, not for the first time, that I live in a building that has one. Walking up several flights of stairs dragging my case would be too much for me today and I'd be tempted to give in to Nigel. As it is, I'm not.

I slump against the side wall of the elevator, not looking back into the lobby. I don't want to see Nigel standing there, wearing whatever expression he's wearing, still holding the flowers.

I'm almost to the door of my apartment when my phone pings again. I pull it out with one hand while I rummage in my bag for my keys with the other.

Nigel: Call me when you change your mind.

His text is followed by a picture of my keys, held against the open door of a taxi.

A hot wash of anger replaces the tightness in my throat.

I start to type out a furious message, then delete it.

At the end of the day, the only person you answer to, is you.

I won't be blackmailed into a relationship. Or into forgiving a shitty Dom.

I flip my phone over and call Blunts.

"Hey, beautiful," Hunter answers. "How was the weekend?"

"Awesome. I owe the Chairman and everyone who came to support me so much. But I've left my keys somewhere, Hunt. My spare set's at the club. Is anyone headed my way in the next couple of hours?"

"Yeah, of course. I'll ask around. If no one's headed your way, I'll bring them myself. I get off in an hour. Be to yours in two. Can you wait that long? You're not out in the hallway, right? You're with a neighbor?"

I am in the hallway. And I'm not friends with any of my neighbors—because I don't want them asking questions about what I do or who I'm with—which is why my spare keys are at Blunts.

"I'll knock on a couple of doors, see if anyone's home. Don't worry about me. Just text when you're on your way, okay? Love you, Hunt."

"Love you, too, beautiful, see you—uh, hold on."

I wait during a muffled discussion. Then Master Javier's voice comes on the line. "You're locked out, mon chou?"

"Yes, sir, but it's fine. I'm safe. I'll be okay for a couple of hours. I have a book—"

"Hunter, address."

I hear Hunter's voice in the background as he reads out my address.

"I'll be there in twenty minutes. Hunter, call me a cab."

"Sir, I don't want to make you take a cab," I protest.

"You're not making me do anything. Do you have adequate water?"

"Yes, sir. I have a water bottle."

"Good. Hang up. Hunter is going to call you back and stay on the line with you until I arrive."

"I promise I'm safe, Master Javier."

Well, mostly safe. We've occasionally had homeless people in the building since the front door is just a buzz through during the day and there's no one manning a security desk or anything like that. I can't afford a building like that.

"Mmm. In a hallway. The circumstances of which we will discuss when I get there since I know you didn't leave your keys anywhere. You're much too careful for that. I'll see you in twenty minutes. Hang up now."

"Yes, sir."

I hang up, smiling at the high-handedness of Doms.

Is it stupid that Master Javier's pushiness makes me feel a hundred times more loved and cared for than Nigel's flowers?

Hunter calls me back.

"He wouldn't do that for me, you know," Hunt says grumpily.

"You wouldn't lose your keys. And yes, he would. And he better be out of hearing range."

"I waited until the door was shut."

"You're taking your hide in your hands, lover boy. I wouldn't be at all surprised if he has the whole place wired."

Hunter groans. "You're probably right. Did you really lose your keys? You should have seen Master Javier's face when he overheard our convo. Aneurism city."

I giggle. I can imagine the normally stoic Dom turning purple.

"No, I didn't lose them. Nigel's an asshole. Let's talk about other shit. Gimme the goss. What happened at the club this weekend?"

"Ooo, baby. If you've been out of the loop, let me tell you the tea."

Hunter keeps me giggling until my phone pings with a text from Master Javier, telling me he's downstairs. I say goodbye to my partner in tattle and drag my bags back into the elevator and downstairs.

Master Javier's blood pressure shoots up a notch when he sees me pulling my big case into the lobby. His swarthy cheeks flush and a vein in his temple pulses.

He holds my spare keys out, then extends an imperious hand. I don't even blink before I take my keys and hand him my bags.

"Thank you, sir."

"You're welcome, ma belle."

I lead the way back into the elevator and up to my apartment. We're not alone in the elevator after the second floor, so neither of us say anything, standing silently side by side. Master Javier waits until I unlock my apartment and he wheels my luggage inside.

He slips his hand under my chin and lifts my face. "If you've been drinking your water like a good girl, you'll need the bathroom."

I do.

"Please, sir."

"Good. Freshen up as well if you need it. You have ten minutes. Have you eaten?"

"No, sir."

"Am I disrupting any plans you have for the evening if I order us dinner?"

I bite my lips because they're going to quiver. This is what I want all the time. Nigel didn't even ask; he just assumed he could commandeer my evening. Why doesn't a Dom like Master Javier want me for their own?

"No, sir."

"Excellent. Would you like wine or spirits with dinner?"

"Wine, please." If we have wine with dinner, Master Javier won't scene with me afterwards. Or during. "Master Javier, would you like to stay?"

He strokes his fingertips down my throat. "Yes, trésor. I'd be happy to stay. No wine with dinner, then, but maybe a bottle for dessert later after we've had a stern discussion about your keys."

The skin under his fingertips goes hot. "I didn't lose them."

"I know you didn't."

"Nigel took them. He was trying to blackmail me into forgiving him for abandoning me this weekend."

Master Javier huffs out a breath. "I understand from Chess that he didn't see fit to honor his financial obligation to you this weekend, either."

My face flares again but I hold his eyes. Master Javier knows all about my money problems and he's never criticized or belittled me, just encouraged me to let the club's financial wizards teach me how to do better. "No, sir."

"May I assume that the two of you are no longer dating or is this just a bump in the road?"

I square my shoulders. "We're no longer dating. You told me the only person I answer to at the end of the day is myself. I need to start making myself happy. Nigel's not making me happy."

He flicks his thumb under my chin. "Good girl. I'm proud of you for putting your happiness first. Unlock your phone and leave it with me while you freshen up. I'll ensure you have your keys back within the hour."

I pull out my phone, unlock it, pull up Nigel's contact, and leave it in Master Javier's hands. I don't know what he'll say to get Nigel to return the keys, but I know Master Javier will get it done.

In my tiny bathroom, I look at myself in the mirror I've mounted on the wall over the sink. Have I done the right thing? Have I been strong and independent or have I thrown away something that wasn't perfect but might have been good if I'd worked harder at it? Have I fallen back on what's safe instead of pushing myself?

My reflection doesn't give me any answers. But the stress lines that were beginning to carve my forehead before this weekend have smoothed out, despite Nigel's assholism over the last hour.

I take that as answer enough.

I wash up, scrub the hours of travel off my teeth, brush and oil my hair until it hangs in soft waves the way Master Javier likes it. I strip down to a black cami and thong, fold my clothes, and carry them out into the bedroom. I don't have a Blunts basque set here at home, since the club provides us with lockers and a free dry-cleaning service for our uniforms. The cami and thong are the closest I have here. So I can answer the door when the food's delivered, I pull on one of the white dress shirts Cappa's left in my closet. Rolling up the sleeves, I join Master Javier in my kitchen/dining room/living room.

He's sitting on the couch with my phone to his ear. When he sees me, he smiles and points to the floor at his feet.

I step over to him, careful to put one foot in front of the other, walking the way I've been taught to please my Dom. When I reach him, I curtsy before folding down onto my knees and crossing my wrists at the small of my back. There's a little tug in my shoulders, but I'm so used to this position that my muscles relax into it after only a twinge.

"Nigel, your plans for the evening and your current distance from Fleur's home are inconsequential to me," Master Javier says after listening to whatever my ex-boyfriend is saying for a minute. "Return the keys within the hour, or I'll report the theft to the authorities. I assure you, they will take this very seriously. An official gentleman will call upon you and hold you in very uncomfortable circumstances overnight. Your time is better spent returning the keys."

I hear a high-pitched squawk and rapid-fire words but I don't try to make out what Nigel's saying. Instead, I look into Master Javier's calm face, his steady eyes, and sink down into the comfort and security of his dominance.

He leans forward to stroke his hand over my hair. The repetitive motion helps me sink. Everything in me, all the questions and doubts and unresolved feelings, smooth into stillness. The peace I feel when I craft my scary boys drapes over me like a weighted blanket.

Master Javier has a few more exchanges with Nigel before he hangs up and sets my phone aside.

"Your keys will be returned shortly. We have twenty minutes before the food arrives. I'm going to fuck your face before we eat, mon petit chaton, but if you want to talk for a few minutes, I can be quick."

I open my mouth and hold my tongue out.

Master Javier smiles and drops a kiss on my forehead before standing and unbuckling his belt. He likes a messy blowjob, but I'm guessing he won't want my lipstick and spit all over his trousers when he doesn't have a change here, so I hold position even as my tongue begins to dry. He peels his trousers and boxers down to his thighs and opens his waistcoat and dress shirt.

I let my eyes drift up from his corded thighs past his long cock to his veined Adonis belt. His body is the last thing you notice about Master Javier. His personality is so forceful, it's hard to see anything else. Then there are his fathomless eyes, full of intelligence and biting wit. If you've known him for a while, you might get to his fleeting smile. I know a lot of submissives who will do anything to win that smile. And if you somehow dig beyond all of that, you get to his trim body. He likes to joke that he keeps in shape by smacking asses, but now that I've been using the club pool to rehab my foot, I know that he swims for an hour a day, every day.

Master Javier is the total package. Any submissive would be lucky to catch his interest and wear his collar. He's collared a couple of different submissives exclusively over the years, but he's very much catch and release. After about a year, he places them with another Dom. He does it carefully, kindly, even genteelly. I've never heard any of them say a bad word about him afterwards.

As much as I'd love to wear Master Javier's collar, I don't want to be someone he releases after a year and places with a substitute Dom. I know myself well enough to know I wouldn't recover from that. When I give my Dom my whole heart, when I fully commit to someone, I want them to commit back.

I want the dream.

But as much as my friend Brenna is living the dream and it looks like Tessa might soon, too, I don't think the dream ever becomes reality for someone like me. I'm too wary. Too skittish. I've seen too much. I've been let down too many times.

So instead, I find another Nigel, a pretty package with a hollow core. I make do with Cappa, knowing that he'll never be satisfied with me so I'll never have to fully commit to him.

I sabotage myself and sabotage myself some more.

Master Javier slides his hand under my chin. "Are you with me, Fleur?"

I wasn't. I was miles away. I shake my head, admitting my distraction. Knowing it will earn me a punishment. Maybe that's what I need now. To hurt and clear out all the shit whirling around in my head and heart.

"You know how I feel about your mind wandering during a scene." He waits until I nod, his eyes darkening, burning. "Do you have any canes here?"

I nod. I have a lot of toys here. Most of them were purchased in the hopes that my Doms would use them on me. Many of them are still in their boxes.

"We'll make use of them later. This will be rough, ma fleur. Slap my hip three times if you need me to stop. You may break position without consequence for that and that only."

I nod, my chin patting against his palm.

"Good." He cups his long, curved cock in his hand and guides the tip into my mouth. His other hand lands on the top of my head, holding me steady. He pushes straight across my tongue and to the back of my mouth on the first thrust. A quick withdrawal to let me breathe and then he's down again, his glans hitting my tonsils. I swallow to avoid gagging and because he likes that sensation around his cockhead. His groan is high praise and I sink back down into that peaceful place where nothing matters but the moment and pleasing my Dom.

I give him my everything, looking up at him as my vision blurs and my eyes stream from the lack of air. Swallowing hard every time he pushes deep to magnify his pleasure. I don't worry about anything. I'll breathe when he lets me. I'll choke when he pounds too deep, too fast. I'll open my throat and let him push all the way down until my nose is buried in his tightly-trimmed curls and my jaw feels like it is splitting in half and it's all beautiful, all good because I'm drawing those deep, approving groans out of him. That's all that matters in this moment.

His cock kicks in my mouth and a hint of saline burns up into my sinuses as he finishes, pumping a few wet strokes followed by dry ones, which tells me this isn't the first time he's come today. He still stretches it out, holding himself down my throat, holding my eyes, while his burn with that dark pleasure.

He slides out of my mouth and immediately cups my chin. "Ma belle fleur, stay with me. You're too deep."

I blink up at him, not understanding.

He wipes my face with a linen hanky, dabbing away tears and

spit. Then he crouches in front of me, cradling my head in his hands. "Count backwards with me. Cinq."

"Cinq."

I count with him, watching his lips form each word and repeating it dutifully. It's what my Dom wants of me in this moment and that's all that matters.

"Tell me your name and address."

I try. I say my name. But my address floats off into the peaceful haze.

"Ah, my dear, you're still so deep. Put your hands in mine and come up on the couch with me."

I do. He guides me until my head's in his lap. I pull my knees up, since the couch is too short to stretch out. Master Javier strokes my head. "Shall I read you a poem, trésor? Or can you tell me about this weekend? I hear it was a great success."

"Whatever you want, Master Javier."

"Perhaps a poem now and the weekend report over dinner." He adjusts his clothes and pulls out his phone. The poem's in French. I can speak a little but not enough to really understand it. I just listen to the sound of his deep, rich voice. My body grows heavy, all the way from my toes to my eyelids, and I drift, wrapped in words from the language of love.

A buzzing startles me awake. A heavy hand cups my shoulder and keeps me from bolting upright.

"Easy, easy. It's just the food arriving. Let me get the door while you sit up slowly. Count of five."

"Yes, sir." I lift my head so he can rise and by the time he brings a fragrant bag back from the front door, I'm sitting up. Nothing hurts. All the little aches of the expo are gone. Even my ankle, which gripes if I'm on it for too long, feels whole. I'm so light.

"There's a lovely smile, flower," Master Javier says. "Nice to see. When you feel steady, go to the linen closet and bring back a towel. I think I'd enjoy this most with you kneeling next to my chair so I can feed you from my hand."

Linen closet? I have a wire rack from a box store that I screwed into the wall above the toilet in my bathroom to hold my towels. It's a jabbing reminder of how far my world is from Master Javier's. I know he's wealthy. One look at his clothes would tell anyone that. But he never acts like his money makes him superior. Master Javier is superior because he's Master Javier, not because of his bank balance.

I bring the towel and set it down on the floor next to the chair at my small dinette table. I settle onto my knees, tuck my hands behind me, and wait.

Master Javier strokes my head between plating out the food. I don't ask what he's bought. It smells good. It's something Asian, with strong ginger and lemongrass smells. Master Javier sits in the chair, tears something into smaller pieces, and holds a piece to my lips.

I take it and chew and savor the peanutty tenderness of the satay. "Thank you, sir."

"You're very welcome. How are you feeling now?"

I swallow before answering. "Light and peaceful, sir."

He smiles at me and feeds me another piece of satay. "That's excellent, ma fleur. Although you drifted off when you should have been focused on me and are due some discipline, I think we'll save that until our usual appointment. I like your current headspace. A relaxed evening with some wine after dinner and another nice, hard fuck before bed will keep you in that headspace better than discipline. Besides." His smile turns wicked. "I do prefer the Delrin for discipline."

I shiver. "Yes, sir."

He pats my head. "You really are a very good girl. I'm sorry about the unpleasantness with Nigel. Perhaps you might find everything you need in the club for a while, mmm? If we met twice a week until Christmas, would that help?"

I look up into his eyes. He's such a good Dom.

"Thank you for everything, Master Javier. I appreciate you – I know you try so hard to help everyone. But I don't think that would help me. I know a lot of people say the best way to get over someone is to get under someone else. I think that will just make me fixate on you. I love you, Master Javier." When his lips purse, I continue quickly, "Please don't take that the wrong way. I love you, but I'm not *in love* with you. You'll always be someone I respect and care for. But I couldn't be your submissive; it would break me when you let me go."

His mouth tips down at the edges. "I know, dearest. That's why I've never offered you my collar."

"I think I need to do this my own way. I need to come to terms with the fact that I'm never going to find what I need most. Instead of sabotaging myself by settling for things that make me happy in the moment but make me miserable the next day, I need to create my own happiness."

"Creating your own happiness is a very worthwhile pursuit. I'm also resigned to the fact that I will never find what I need most. There is no perfect person for me. I'd like to believe there is a perfect Dom for you, though, flower. Let me persist in my delusion for a little while, hum? And let me stand in for him until you find him?"

I smile, shaking my head. "Why is there a perfect Dom for me but no perfect subbie for you, sir?"

"Because I was born with only half a heart. Something the men in my family all suffer from, a terrible missing piece that requires absolute perfection to fill. And when we fill it with anything else, we sour. We rot from the inside out until nothing's left but bitterness and cruelty. I saw it with my father and my father's father and my brother. I don't want to become that sort of monster. So as soon as I feel the first drop of bitterness, I help that sweet, shining creature who has given herself to me with such devotion find a better man. Someone who will love all her perfect imperfections, instead of growing to hate her for them." His smile is so sad that it takes all my willpower not to break position and hug him. "You are nothing like me. You have a full heart, full of love. You just need to find someone strong enough to suffer your love, Fleur. Love is not always easy and gentle. You and I both know that love can be dark and harsh. I believe you will find someone who won't just endure your love, they'll revel in it. Crave it. Do anything for it. Don't give up, dearest."

"Master Javier, can I please hug you?"

His smile brightens and he opens his arms. "Of course. Come here, trésor."

I climb up into his lap and hug him tightly. He hugs me back and rocks me and when my arms loosen a little, he starts feeding me again, still sitting in his lap where I'm cherished and at peace.

The fact that I'm not perfect doesn't bother me. I know I'm not. Trying to be perfect for Master Javier would only hurt us both. That he can be so honest with me soothes any sting. That he believes there's someone out there for me gives me that flicker of hope to keep looking tomorrow.

[The End]

NINE

a tumorous tail

*MASTER BULL, KINKY KIKI, QUEEN TWITCH,
AND GUEST – GEORGIE*

MASTER BULL HOLDS his finger to his lips.

The gesture is kind of a waste on me. I'm a mouse. If there's something I know how to be, it's quiet.

But I'd never disagree with a master.

He takes my coat and hat, waits while I fluff my fur, then gestures me to follow.

I creep after him, up the stairs of his very nice modern apartment onto the second floor. I haven't been in many places this nice. It has marble floors in the entryway and a huge sparkling chandelier hanging over the staircase we're sneaking up.

Music's playing from one of the upstairs rooms. It's not quite what I'd expect in this mini-palace of marble and glass. It's sweet and somehow earthy: pipes and drums and strings and a chorus of voices singing a song that sounds traditional but I don't recognize it from my parents' church or school or anything. Over the music there's a whirring, mechanical sound. That I do recognize. A sewing machine.

I have one, too. I quickly realized that if I didn't make my own outfits, expressing my mouse-soul was going to bankrupt me.

Bull leads me down a hallway. The ceiling is high and arched overhead. Beneath my paws, the floor's padded by a thick, teal-and-pink carpet that looks like it was just installed and no one's ever walked on it. Big pieces of glass art, lit from within and glowing like a sunset, decorate the walls. I shrink into myself even smaller, not wanting to brush anything with my paws or furry shoulders. This place is like a museum.

There's a closed door at the end of the hallway, and a door that's cracked open just before the end. It's from the slightly open door that the music and mechanical sounds are coming.

Master Bull holds up a finger and pokes his head around the door, so whoever is inside can't see me.

"Twitch, time for a break," he says, his deep voice muffled by whatever is in that room.

"Five minutes," responds a cheerful tenor voice. It rejoins the chorus. "My love said to me, a-ley, a-ley, a-ley-de-ai. I cannot come with thee, a-ley, a-ley, a-ley-de-ai."

A funny longing builds in my chest. I've never heard the song before, but it makes me *want* something. I'm not sure exactly what. I don't know how to get it. But I want it.

"Now, Twitch. I'm going to wake Kiki and then I have a surprise for both of you, so if you're not in my bedroom, on your knees, by the time I'm ready for you, we'll start with ten stripes and go from there."

I shiver and back away a step. I've only had play Doms, never a Master of my own, so I don't really know what a permanent, live-in D/s relationship looks like. I probably wouldn't tell my Dom "five minutes," even though I like to brat when I'm in the mood, but never when it would get me stripes of anything. My friend Orca introduced me to Master Bull and vouched for him, but I won't be mouthing off to him. He seems really strict. And like he'd make sure I didn't sit for a week if I said something that really pissed him off.

Master Bull backs out of the room and beckons me after him as he continues down the hallway to the closed door. Behind us, the sewing machine noise starts up again.

Master Bull opens the door at the end of the hallway and walks through. The door beyond is dim and huge, bigger than the kitchen and living room of the apartment I share with my two roommates. It's a bedroom, but it's so big there's a whole library in it with a couch and armchairs. Doors lead off it, probably to a bathroom or walk-in closet. The bed's massive, the biggest I've ever seen, with huge, curving wood pieces at the head and foot and sheer curtains that drape down from the ceiling.

The woman lying in the bed looks tiny in comparison. She stirs and scoots up on the mountain of pillows when Bull walks in.

"Hey, babe," he says, his voice gentle. "Time to wake up. You want any help getting out of bed?"

She shakes her head and smooths the covers over her legs. She's wearing a nightgown fit for a princess, in a teal that matches the deep purple, teal, and pink décor.

"I was actually awake," she says. "I definitely have more energy."

Bull sits on the edge of the bed and takes one of her hands. The bones are sharp under her skin, but her grip looks solid.

"That's great, babe," Bull says. "I brought you a gift."

He beckons me forward with two fingers.

I drop to my hands and knees, scuttle over to the bed, and peep over the edge.

The woman's eyes go wide, and soft as fur. "Aren't you the most adorable thing?" she coos. "Do you have a name?"

Since Master Bull told me to be quiet and I prefer not to talk in scenes when I'm in mouse-form, I nod.

"This is Georgie. I know how much you miss not having pets since I'm allergic. Happy birthday, babe."

"Oh, sir." She slides closer to him and wraps her arms around him. "Thank you so much."

"Georgie loves having their ears and fur stroked," Master Bull tells her. "I want to watch them eat you out while I spend some quality time with Twitch. He's asking for some stripes."

"And the boot," the woman purrs. "He's forgotten where he belongs."

"Couldn't agree more," Master Bull says. "You get acquainted with Georgie. I'll get changed. Twitch comes in while I'm in the closet, tell him to strip and get in position three on the damn floor."

"Yes, Master." She slides back into the pillows and wiggles her fingers at me as Bull stands and moves away from the bed. "Would you like to come up on the bed, precious?"

I nod eagerly and scramble up onto the bed. I curl by her hip. Her hands immediately sink into my fur and begin stroking over the top of my head and down the back of my neck.

"I'm Kiki, you beautiful thing," she coos. "You've met Bull and Twitch. Twitch is in trouble, but don't worry about what you see. We've been together for years. Bull knows what Twitch needs, even if it looks harsh. And Twitch has a safe word. We all do. Do you have a safe word, precious?"

I nod and let out the three, high squeaks combined with three pats to her thigh that form my safe word.

"Got it," she says, still stroking. "That's good. I always feel better playing with a safe word. I don't want you worrying about anything. Just so you know, I've been sick, but it's nothing catching. I had cancer but I'm in remission and I'm doing much better lately."

Poor woman. I make a soft, sad squeak and stroke her thigh through the blankets.

"Bull's so good to me," Kiki says, letting her fingers wander through the fur down my back. "Sensation play is my favorite and you are such a sensory delight. So soft. The fur on your neck is like down."

She plays with it, smiling down at me. She's pretty, even with her cheeks hollow and eyes sunken. There's still a glow about her, the glow of someone who is well-loved and knows it.

The door out into the hallway flies open and a person strides through. They're tall, slender; they place one foot in front of the other in a line like they're chewing up a catwalk with their long legs. They're wearing a dark blue denim pants suit with a bright orange, silk tee under the fitted jacket. Silver-gray hair flows around sculpted cheeks and jaw. Perched on top of the pale waves is a winking, gold tiara.

"Darling," the person says as they stride across the carpet. "Tell me you were awake when he crashed in here."

Kiki nods. "He says get naked and get in position three."

The person stops like they've hit a wall. They stroke their throat with coffin nails painted like a sunset with black French tips.

"Goddess, yes," they say. "And who is that cute thing in bed with you?"

"This is Georgie," Kiki says. "Georgie's going to have fun with me while Master takes you in hand."

The person—is their name really Twitch?—shrugs out of their jacket, folds it and lays it in one of the armchairs.

"Perfect," Twitch says. "Georgie, you take good care of my Kinky Kiki. She deserves all the good things. And I deserve all the bad ones."

The way they roll *bad ones* tells me Twitch doesn't think they're bad at all.

Twitch finishes undressing, placing their crown carefully on top of the pile of folded clothes, revealing long, lightly tanned limbs, a flat chest, G-string cupping a heavy package, suspenders and what look like silk stockings. Twitch leaves the G-string, suspenders and stockings on as they fold themselves to the floor. They settle onto elbows and knees and press their forehead to the carpet. Goosebumps rise on the warm golden skin of Twitch's back. Are they listening, waiting to hear the footfall of their master? Are they nervous? Is that why goosebumps are rising? Or just so excited that adrenaline is pumping under their skin?

The footfalls, when they come, are heavy, clomping, even if muffled by the carpet. Master Bull walks through one of the doors opening off the bedroom. He's naked except for a pair of black boots that lace up his shins.

I blink a few times, not quite believing what I'm seeing.

Master Bull's dick hangs all the way down to his knees. All the way. I've never seen a dick so long. How do his submissives take that thing? I shudder and curl more tightly against Kiki's leg.

She laughs softly and rubs her fingertips up and down my back, ruffling my fur. "He looks scary, doesn't he? I'd say he's really a teddy bear, but he's not. He's patient, though. He trained us both to take him."

I gulp and nod. I hope that's not expected of me. When I met Bull for coffee at the restaurant of Blunts—a club I'd give not one but both of my testicles to be part of—he said he was looking for a furry to please his partner and that I'd only be giving her oral in this scene. But if it went well, we could talk about more in the future. I'd be interested in that, but not if it means training my throat or ass to take Bull's monster.

Bull strides over to where Twitch is kneeling. He lifts his left foot and places the heel on the back of Twitch's silver-gray head.

"You've been out of line, pup," Bull growls to his submissive.

I shiver uncontrollably and paw at Kiki's thigh. She gives her own shiver as she draws my velvet tail through her hands.

"Takes more than ten percent of your attention to keep me in line," Twitch says, their voice muffled by the carpet. "And that's all you've been giving me."

"We've both had other things on our minds," Bull says. "But now you've got my full attention. Lift your head and lick my boot, pup. Show me you're still mine."

"Can you still handle me, sir?" Twitch says.

"Oh, I can handle you." Taking his boot off Twitch's head, Bull goes down on one knee, gathers those silvery waves in one big hand, and pulls Twitch's head back. It would be painful even to watch, but Twitch is wholly relaxed in Bull's grasp. They moan softly.

"Yes, master."

"That's right. You like it when I take you in hand." Bull lowers Twitch's head to the carpet and presses down, then pulls back again. "Lick my boot."

Twitch turns his head, which Bull's hold allows but it must be pulling on Twitch's scalp like a bitch. Twitch's face doesn't show a flicker of pain, though. The muscles are relaxed, even as the skin's drawn tight by Bull's hold. Twitch's long, pale pink tongue flicks out. The pointed tip swirls leisurely over the black, leather toe of Bull's boot, then down along the stitched seam between leather and sole.

"That's right. Good boy. Other side."

Twitch strains to reach the far side of Bull's boot, tendons popping up in Twitch's long neck. Twitch laves the boot leather, leaving shiny streaks.

"Mmm, very good," Bull says. "I'm giving you those ten stripes. You need them. Say you accept them."

Twitch lifts their head slightly. "I accept them, Master."

"That's my pup. What a good boy."

Bull releases Twitch's head. The submissive sags and puts their forehead back down to the carpet.

As Bull heads back into the closet, Kiki pulls the covers aside. "Wasn't that beautiful, Georgie?" she asks.

I nod and shift over so I can lie across her legs, being careful not to rest my full weight on her thin limbs. I'm encouraged when she continues to stroke my head and shoulders.

"I love your colors, Georgie," Kiki says. "Your little pink ears, your gray back and white tummy. You even have a black tip to your tail. So cute."

I wriggle at the praise. My mouse-form can get lost among more flamboyant fursuits. I love it when someone appreciates its natural beauty. I stroke her nightgown up her legs, taking my time, letting my paws linger so she can enjoy the slight roughness of my paw pads against her skin and the contrast of my fur against her skin.

Kiki shifts and I move between her legs so she can lift her knees. I rub my skin-cheek against her thigh. She's soft, too. I've only worn the hood of my fursuit today since I knew we were going to do oral and that's impossible with my mouse-face on.

My attention's drawn away from Kiki when Bull returns with a long, rubbery tube. He uncaps it and pulls out a rattan cane as long as his arm and as thick as his thumb.

"Raise that ass, boy," Bull growls at Twitch.

Twitch's smooth haunches rise a few inches. And sway.

Bull puts his hand on the small of Twitch's back, holding the submissive still. Then the cane falls with a swish and a crack.

Everyone but Bull jumps. Twitch settles back into position with a moan.

Kiki laughs softly. "That makes such a noise. And so does Twitch."

Twitch's moans rise to a low howl over the next several strikes. They stay in position, though. I guess Bull has his submissives well-trained in a lot of aspects.

I get Kiki moaning, too. With licks and nibbles up her smooth thighs. She said she loves sensation play, so I alternate gentle scratching with my little claws and stroking with the furry backs of my paws. Those make her shiver and arch back into the pillows. The warm, bready smell of arousal rises from the V of her pussy. I dip my head and take a taste.

"Oh, Georgie."

She grabs my ears. I reach up and gently untangle her hands. People without fursonas don't understand about pulling on ears. I don't squeak indignantly at her. I just guide her hands away, settling them on my shoulders as I sink down between her thighs for taste after taste.

Her legs fall wide. I explore deeper with my tongue, licking her in time to the cracks of the cane against Twitch's muscled ass.

Kiki's fingers dig into my shoulders as I find the rhythm she likes, fast flicks against her clit and then a deep taste at her center. She writhes beneath me. I slide my hands around the backs of her thighs and grip her ass cheeks. She's soft there, too, with the remnants of what must have been a full, round ass before she got sick. I knead her ass-cheeks, pulling them apart since I figure Bull will have broken her in there and some stimulation will help her get there.

It does. Kiki shudders and bucks as I lick deep into her, then pull back to suck on her clit. She makes a wonderful "woo-woo-woop" sound that makes me grin as I flick my tongue rapidly over her clit. She shakes all over with her climax, her hands flopping down onto the mattress. She calls out my name, Twitch's name, the name of her master, and even though I'm a stranger, I feel a part of their circle just for this moment.

I rest my cheek against her thigh as she comes down from her release.

Bull has finished with Twitch, who is sobbing softly as he licks Bull's other boot, thanking him for the correction. Bull murmurs to Twitch, words too low for me to hear over Kiki's harsh breaths, but whatever he's saying loosens the muscles of Twitch's back until the submissive is slumped bonelessly, their face nestled against their master's boot.

Bull looks up, takes in his other submissive, who is lying back in the pillows, her eyes closed, languidly stroking my head.

Bull smiles at me. "Thank you, Georgie," he mouths, without sound.

I smile back at him, happy to have helped.

[The End]

an eximious tail

MISTRESS MAUDE AND GEORGIE - GEORGIE

THIS PLACE IS OVERWHELMING.

I can hardly believe that I'm allowed *inside* Blunts. I've heard about this place for years, but I never thought I'd step foot through the door. Maybe they'd allow a mouse like me in the nightclub. But never upstairs. Never in their inner sanctum.

I look around the Library, with its two floors and towering stacks of books. With the floor to ceiling windows letting in good light and green lamps on every table in case the day turns gray. The floors are softened with carpets that I can believe came from Persia. Leather wingback chairs are drawn together in cozy clumps and in them sit some of the most respected, most feared dominants in the City.

I do not belong here.

A gentle hand tugs on my wrist. "Come on. Let me show you the stacks."

My self-appointed guide is Emily, the club's only Little and, according to Queen Twitch, an excellent amateur historian. I have one of her newsletters with a story about a war in the 1920s between Blunts and its sister club in New Jersey folded carefully in my backpack. When Emily found out Bull had brought me to play with his trio, she asked Queen Twitch if I would help her research and write an article about furry play.

I had no idea we'd be working in the *club's* library.

"A-are you sure we're allowed?" I whisper.

"Promise," she says, holding up two fingers. "We had our Halloween party in here and people spilled things and *still* no one kicked us out. As long as we don't color on the walls, we're good. I think some of my friends were tempted, though."

I glance at the few walls peeking between the tall stacks. They're wood-paneled to waist-height and papered above.

I totally understand the desire to color on them. I draw good cartoon mice. The walls would look amazing with some cartoon mice peeking out from between the panels.

Following my eyes, Emily giggles. "You really can't. But if you want to draw after, I'll draw with you. I have some art supplies with Twitch's bookbinding stuff."

"Okay," I agree.

Emily leads me up a spiral, wrought-iron staircase. More towering stacks of beautiful books that smell like leather and vanilla. More leather chairs. More beautiful rugs. This place is so intimidating.

I whimper.

A woman sitting in one of the leather chairs looks up from the newspaper she has spread over her knee. The newspaper is pink, paler than the deep rose blouse she wears with a black pencil skirt and high-heeled ankle boots with red soles. Her silver hair is bobbed around her face. She's wearing school-marm glasses with tortoise-shell frames and a gold chain looped around her neck.

She raises an eyebrow that's still a dark brown, touched with frost.

I turn to flee.

"Georgie," Emily says, tugging me toward a long table spread with books. "That's Mistress Maude. She's my friend. She's scary, yes, but she's also lovely. She's happy you're here. Everyone is."

"She doesn't look happy I'm here," I whisper.

"I promise you, she is. We'll probably have lunch with her and Master Javier, who is just as scary but also lovely. I promise, no one will be mean to you. Well, not unless you ask them to be."

I shake my head, feeling my mouse ears catch the air. I've only worn the hood of my fur-suit today, and left the paws in my pockets, so that I can help pull books and write up what we find. I'm also not sure how the people here will take my mouse-face. I haven't seen any other furries since I arrived, so I don't know how used to fursuits the dominants are. I don't want to make a bad impression.

Emily shows me where the diaries and folios about the club's history are kept. I understand why she needs help. There are shelves and shelves. It's barely alphabetized and the folios don't look organized at all.

"I've been trying to do a decade at a time," Emily tells me. "I know it looks like a big ole mess, but it's better than it was, I swear. Twitch only just started two weeks ago. He hasn't gotten to any of this yet, if you can believe it. He's working on the bound volumes that are absolutely falling apart."

I nod, but truthfully, this is all news to me. I've played with Master Bull's trio four times now, but Queen Twitch has a lot of making up to do, so I haven't even gotten to touch the Queen yet, much less have many opportunities to talk to them. I knew Queen Twitch was working at Blunts, in the library, but I didn't realize they were doing book restoration, or that they'd only been here for two weeks.

"If Queen Twitch is so new," I whisper to Emily, "are you sure it's okay I'm here?"

She takes my hand and squeezes. "I promise. I know this place can be overwhelming at first. I was bowled over when Daddy started bringing me here. And even though not everyone is okay with my

Littleness, they're still very kind to me." She grins wickedly. "Daddy punishes them when they're not."

I met Emily's daddy, Master Logan, for the first time this morning. He escorted Emily when she met me at Bull's house and walked me over to the club. Emily did most of the talking, but Master Logan chimed in from time to time. I noticed Master Logan took Emily's hand every time we came to a crosswalk, and that he kept his body between her and the street as we were walking. Those sorts of things probably don't matter to everyone. But I noticed them.

"Your daddy seems nice," I tell Emily.

"He is. Most of the time. But when he's not nice, he's super-scary." She shivers, gripping her elbows. "Getting on Daddy's bad side is something your bottom will never forget."

Some of my nervousness eases and I chuckle.

Emily shows me what she's already assembled about the history of furries at the club. I page through it with interest. Although most people think that furries are a recent thing, I've seen pictures of fursuits and anthropomorphic animals dating back into the Victorian era. There aren't any pictures that old, but there are some from the 1940s. I sort them out of the pile and fan them out to show Emily.

She leans into my shoulder as she looks over what I've assembled. I'm not really used to touch outside of scenes. Lots of people find my fursuit off-putting.

I curl my arm through hers, so she knows her touch is welcome.

She pulls out a black and white picture of a man in a full morning suit, with top hat, tails, and cane. He's also wearing a horse head and a long, silky tail that cascades to the ground between his spats.

"What do you think?" Emily asks me, her voice pitched at library-appropriate-volume.

"I'd call it early furry play," I offer back just as quietly. "It's anthropomorphization. That's the heart of furry play."

"Can I show you where I found it? You might see more than I do."

"Yes, please."

She leads me to a stack beside a window that lets in the crisp morning light. I could tell from the street that the club's windows were treated in some way so people couldn't see in from the street. This window faces the club's inner courtyard and overlooks the restaurant's glass conservatory. Beyond the glittering peaked roof flap the pennants that edge the entry to the Stables. The courtyard's grass is perfectly green and trimmed even though it's November and everywhere else is brown and withered.

A mouse could run around happily in that grass for hours. And play hide and seek in the huge, bushy maze that fills the far end of the courtyard. And bed down for the night, safe and warm, in the Stables.

That's about as likely to happen as I am to turn into a dragon.

With a sigh, I turn back to the untidy piles of paper on the shelves Emily's indicated. I pick up the first pile and page through it. All I find initially are club accounts, handwritten and meticulously kept to the penny. But at the bottom of the stack are pages from the accountant's diary, listing scenes in each of the club's four dungeons. I read through these with interest. When I find references to "pony training," I separate out the diary and set it aside for further review.

I'm reaching for the next stack when a voice as crisp as the November sunlight says, "I wouldn't have thought the club's financial accounts from the 1940s would be relevant to what you're researching, Georgie."

Startled, I squeak and drop the pile of papers.

"Oh, dear." It's the silver-haired woman with the tortoise-shell glasses and stern eyebrow. She holds on to a shelf as she lowers herself to one knee and begins pushing the papers back into a stack.

I squeak again. "Please don't, mistress! I can do this."

I scramble to pick up the spilled papers and as the Domme rises to her feet, I clutch them to my chest and step back from her.

"I'm sorry I startled you, dear," she says.

"My fault, my fault," I hurry to say.

"It wasn't and I'm not so proud that I can't admit when I'm wrong, Georgie. Keeps me humble."

Furious heat rises to my face. Did I imply she was too proud to kneel?

Her eyes drift to my cheeks. Inky pupils expand inside the flinty circles of her irises.

Does she like that I'm turning redder than a strawberry?

She runs a manicured French tip along the edge of the papers I'm holding. "Care to explain what you're looking for?"

"I-I-I'm just looking, mistress."

"It's Mistress Maude, if you're going to call me by my title." She extends a hand. "It's a pleasure to meet you."

I shake, aware that my hand trembles and that many people wipe their palms on their pants after shaking hands with me.

Mistress Maude doesn't.

Her fingers are cool and firm. She holds my hand after shaking, not gripping too hard, but not letting go, either.

"Now that you've relaxed a hair, tell me what you're looking for? I've been using this library for longer than you've been alive, I suspect. I might just be able to assist."

"Oh, yes, of-of-of course, Mistress Maude. I'm helping Emily research early instances of furry play at the club. We've found a picture of an anthropomorphic horse from the 1940s." I set down the pile I've picked up and, fumbling only a little because Mistress Maude is still gently holding my other hand, pick up the accountant's diary. "I found this diary at the bottom of that ledger. It looks like it was kept by the same person. It records all the scenes and there are references to pony training."

"Indeed?" Maude's eyebrow arches over the rim of her glasses again and heat rushes back to my face.

"Yuh-yes, Mistress Maude."

"May I?"

I offer her the papers. She finally releases my hand to leaf through the stack.

I clasp my hands together behind me, wishing I could transfer the contact of her skin on mine to my other hand to recreate that warm, reassuring sensation.

"Mmm, here's one that's interesting." She shifts to my side so she can show me a page. She underlines an entry with her fingernail. "Farming: milking the cow, currying the horse, breeding."

"Yes, ma'am."

Her cool, grey-blue eyes lift to mine. It only hits me then than she's an inch or two shorter than I am. She has such a commanding presence it's surprising she doesn't tower over me.

"I've watched a great deal of furry play, Georgie. I don't know if you're aware, but Blunts has a relationship with the Elephant's Playground. We host play nights for them regularly."

I nod. "Yes, ma'am. That's how I met Master Bull. I've only gone to a few of their events and never one of the play nights here, ma'am. But J.R. from Elephant's Playground recommended me when Master Bull contacted them, looking for a pet for Miss Kiki."

Her gaze sharpens. "I see."

A shudder works down my spine. "Ha-have I done something wrong, Mistress Maude?"

"No, Georgie. May I touch you?"

She wants to touch me? My chest seizes.

"Please just don't pull on my ears."

"Of course not." She strokes a hand down my arm, smoothing down my fur. Is it vain to hope she feels the muscles under my fursuit? "Have you been playing with Bull, Kiki, and Twitch? You don't have to answer if the question's impertinent."

"It's naw-not impertinent, ma'am. And yes, I've played with them a few times."

She hums in her throat. I'm not sure if that's a good hum or a bad one. I'm glad I'm not wearing my mouse face because my whiskers would be shaking like leaves in a hurricane.

"While I don't condone the poaching of submissives, I would

very much like to scene with you, Georgie," she says. "Do I need to ask for Bull's consent before I invite you to scene with me?"

The ball of nerves that my chest has been contracting around drops into my stomach. And sends a tingle through my balls. This elegant, fearsome woman wants to scene with me?

How do I answer her? Yes? No? I have no idea what the etiquette is here. I haven't made any commitment to Master Bull and his partners, but we've already scheduled our next play session for the weekend. I'd be a little heartbroken if they canceled; maybe I've made a commitment to them in my head?

"I-I-I'm not sure, ma'am, but I'd like to let Master Bull know."

She tips her head. "Very diplomatic, Georgie. I think that's wise. I'll step out and give him a call now, if you don't mind, while you keep on with your good work. I planned to join you and Emily for lunch anyway. If Bull's amenable, do you have time for a scene this afternoon?"

I can't stop my head from bobbing madly.

She laughs throatily and strokes her cool fingers down my cheek before she passes me the papers she's holding, turns on her red-soled heel, and walks away.

Leaving me to stumble back to the table where Emily's working, holding my papers in a jittering hand, my stomach rioting, my blood racing, to try to concentrate—somehow—until I see Mistress Maude again.

[The end . . . for now.]

a fluffleous tail

CHAIRMAN CHESS, MISTRESS MAUDE, MISS GINGER, LITTLES' ARMY, ALLYN, TESSA, AND GEORGIE - GEORGIE

THE TINY BALL of grey and white fluff on the grass glares at me with eyes like honed steel.

It jerks. It's hind feet thwap ringingly on the ground.

"Oh, dear," Miss Ginger says, her voice rich with laughter. "Someone's feeling feisty."

I move my gaze from the furious creature at my feet to Robin's Mommy. She's smiling as she looks at me but I quiver, worried I've done something wrong.

"What does it want?" I whisper.

My friend Emily looks up from where she's sitting with three balls of fluff in her lap. One of them is asleep as she strokes between its floppy ears. Another is chewing on a strawberry top. The third is stretched out beside her knee, lazily licking its front paw.

None of them are glaring and thumping at her.

"What have I done?" I ask no one and everyone.

A hand as warm and gentle as Emily's runs over my furhood,

between my ears. "Relax, Georgie," Mistress says. *Mistress Maude.* Not my Mistress. "You haven't done anything wrong. The bunny might not like you looming over it. You're very big to it."

How can I be big to a bunny? I'm a mouse.

"Come sit by me," Emily calls to me, patting the grass beside her with her free hand.

Mistress Maude squeezes my shoulder reassuringly.

Even though I don't want to leave the comfort of her touch, I scurry to Emily's side and sit cross-legged in the grass.

The grey and white bunny hops after me, positions herself in front of me again, and thumps.

"Why is she *doing* that?" I whisper to Emily.

Lacey, the red-haired lady from New Jersey who brought the dozen bunnies Blunts bought to be a therapy herd, squats in the grass behind the grey and white bunny. She offers her fingers to the bunny. The bunny sniffs, whiskers shaking, then thumps again.

"Hmm," says Lacey. "This is Cupcake. She's an extremely dominant bunny. Very dominant females don't always take well to being moved. It might take a couple of days for her to settle in."

"Very like people," Mistress Maude says, smiling her medium smile. In the few days since she approached me in the Library, I've learned all her smiles. This is polite and open, unlike her little smile which is wry, or her big smile which rolls into a chuckle.

"And I see half our boys have found you, Emily," Lacey says, grinning. "This is Fountain. He's still growing into his bladder, so leave him on the grass instead of putting him in your lap." She pets the bunny lying beside Emmy's knee. "This is Chex, because he looks like Chex-mix." She strokes the bunny eating the strawberry who has a brindled brown coat. "And this is our beautiful little Rex. He could be a show bunny. He's got the body and the coat. But he's so mild-tempered I think he'll do better as a therapy bunny." She pets the sleeping bunny in Emily's lap, who doesn't even twitch.

Cupcake, evidently taking umbrage at all the attention not directed at her, thumps three times.

Lacey laughs.

Cupcake pivots so her back is to Lacey and she's shooting me furious side-eye.

I hold up my paws. I haven't petted the other bunnies. I don't deserve her ire.

"I shouldn't laugh at her. Bunnies are very sensitive to being laughed at. But they're such little divas sometimes." Lacey offers her fingers to Cupcake again. Lacey's brave. I wouldn't put my fingers that close to angry bunny teeth. Cupcake sniffs and thumps. "Oh, I'm really in trouble. She usually puts her head down for grooming after a couple of thumps."

"I read that's how the pecking order works in a bunny herd," Cynnie says as she joins us in the grass. She has her own armful of bunny, a black and white bunny who has grass sticking out of both sides of its mouth as it chews. "The dominant bunny puts its head down and the submissive bunny licks the dominant bunny."

"That's right," Lacey says, her tone approving.

"*Very* like people," Emily chirps. Everyone chuckles.

Cupcake shifts a little closer to my crossed legs. Is she going to bite me? I'm wearing my fursuit, but I've seen the bunnies yawn while Lacey's been getting them settled in their new hutches and big, grassy run. Their teeth are *terrifying*.

"Miss Lacey," another of Emily's friends, Sammi, pipes up. Sammi's not allowed to hold the bunnies. Evidently there was an incident at the zoo. But Sammi has his own fluffy friend. A tiny goat that's barely bigger than the bunnies follows Sammi everywhere. When Sammi plops in the grass, the goat plops down beside him, folding its legs beneath it so it looks like bread loaf with very small horns. "Won't the bunnies get cold? Shouldn't they live inside?"

"No, Sammi," Lacey explains. "Bunnies are adapted to live outside. They've already started growing thick, warm coats for the winter. That's why they feel so soft. The hutches give them the same sort of protection they'd have in their dens in the wild. As long as they have plenty of hay to burrow in, they'll be very comfortable out here. This is a great enclosure for them." She looks around the annex that's been built off the Stables for Harry-the-Mini Goat and the bunnies. It has an opaque glass roof to let the light in, but the sides are canvas. "Lots of space to run around. Out of the elements. The threat to rabbits isn't cold so much as wet. If they get soaked all the way through to their undercoats, they can't regulate their body temperature and can get pneumonia. So it's important they have somewhere sheltered and dry. Although plenty of rabbits enjoy getting wet and I've seen rabbits swim in ponds and streams. Never put them in a chlorinated pool, though. Their skin is sensitive."

The handful of Littles, plus the pony-boy Allyn, who has volunteered to be the primary caretaker for the bunnies and Harry, nod together.

"We could build a little pool for them to swim in, Mistress Maude," Allyn says, looking up at her.

"With a fountain, for Fountain," Emily giggles.

"Harry would like a fountain. He could drink out of it," Sammi says, bouncing on his butt. Harry bounces up next to him like the little goat's on strings, boings several times, then folds himself back down. Sammi wraps his arms around his goat's neck and squeezes.

"Gently, Sammi," Mommy Ginger reminds the Little.

Sammi immediately loosens his hold. Harry evidently doesn't hold strangulation against his friend and butts his nose against Sammi's side.

"I'll speak with Chess about it," Mistress Maude says, without promising, but she's smiling her big smile.

She should look out of place here. Among bunnies and littles, a goat and a furson. But Mistress Maude's presence is so authoritative, she shapes everything around her to fit. In the Library, she fit in her pencil skirt and red-soled boots. In the dungeon, she fit in her satin and lace. Here, she fits in her tailored khaki trousers and knee-high, deep green gum boots. But it's more than her wearing the right outfit for each occasion. It's that sense of calm authority. She's unflappable, when I'm so easily . . . flapped.

As though she's conjured him, the club's chairman, Chess, comes through the door from the Stables. He's a big man, although he cloaks his muscles under expensively tailored suits; I can see the strength in his thick neck, the heavy thigh muscles that move under the fine wool. His face is as smooth as his clothes, but he wears grief in the faint lines around his eyes and crossing his forehead. Pure dominance shines in his dark eyes. I don't know how the pretty, smiling submissive, dressed in ears, a face mask, paws, and tail for puppy play, gracing his arm stands being near him. He's suffocating.

"How are we doing, Lacey?" he asks. He pauses near the door, taking a chain lead out of his pocket and clipping it to his submissive's collar. She drops onto all fours and when he starts off again, her lead wrapped around his hand, she follows.

My stomach does a slow roll. I've seen plenty of pet play. I know submissives enjoy acting like ponies, puppies, kitties, and other animals for their dominants. But I can't help wondering, if this is what the Blunts dominants expect, what will they think of me? I'm not a pet. I'm a furson.

They won't understand. They won't like me once they really understand.

If they understand.

I should hide my mouse-soul. I should behave the way they expect a pet to behave.

Mistress's hand closes on my shoulder at the same moment Cupcake hops into the open space between my crossed legs.

"Oh!"

"Try offering her your fingers to sniff," Mistress Maude suggests, giving my shoulder a squeeze.

"What if she bites me?" I whisper.

"Then it's a good thing I was a nurse for ten years before I moved into administration," Mistress says. "I'll take very good care of you, Georgie."

Heat runs straight down my spine.

The rabbit between my knees glares and thumps.

Mistress chuckles. "Jealous little thing."

The warmth of her hand slides away.

"Like this, Georgie," Lacey says, offering her fingers, held out flat, to the bunny in Cynnie's lap. The bunny sniffs, then lowers its head. Lacey strokes gently up and down its nose with one finger.

Shaking, I extend my palm to Cupcake.

She's going to bite me. She's going to bite me.

She puts her head down.

Copying Lacey, I rub the tip of my finger up and down Cupcake's nose.

"She's so soft," I say in wonder. I've never touched a real rabbit before. They don't feel like cats or dogs or fursons. It's like stroking a warm cloud.

"Just like you, Georgie," Mistress says softly behind me. Her fingers run down the back of my neck. I've worked on my fursuit for years, finding the softest fake fur, learning how to care for it so it stays sleek and pillowy. Does she like touching it?

With everything in me, I hope so.

"Most bunnies like their heads, shoulders, and backs touched," Lacey tells us as I take my cautious strokes up between Cupcake's alert ears. "They get nervous if you touch their sides, haunches, or tails. And you've won them over completely if they let you touch their bellies."

Would Cupcake ever let me stroke her belly? I don't think so.

I keep petting Cupcake's head while Lacey passes around very small hairbrushes and shows us how to brush the rabbits. Chairman Chess tries to brush the bunny in Cynnie's lap, but gets thumped at, to his surprise. The Littles snigger and giggle at the disgruntlement on the big man's face as he passes the brush back to Cynnie. Her bunny settles back down once she starts brushing it.

"I see rabbits are just as unruly as submissives," Chess grumps.

Lacey laughs. "They can be very picky about who they accept grooming from. I suspect Bobbi doesn't believe you're submitting."

Tessa, Chess's puppy, wheezes with laughter.

"Well," Chess allows, "Bobbi might be right."

Cupcake suddenly stiffens under my fingers like she's had a seizure and flops over onto her side, her back pressing against my shins.

"Oh, no," I moan. "She's hurt. I've done something to hurt her. I swear I didn't touch her anywhere but her head."

Mistress's hand closes around the back of my neck. "It's okay, Georgie."

Lacey laughs warmly. "Cupcake's just getting comfortable. When bunnies are very happy and relaxed, they flop over like that. She might dig her head under your leg a little. It's okay if she does."

As though she's following Lacey's suggestion, Cupcake's bull-dog-shaped head nudges under my calf. I hold myself as still as possible, still afraid of hurting her if I move incautiously.

Mistress's hand moves down my neck. Her palm slides warmly back and forth across my shoulders. "Relax, Georgie. You're not hurting the bunny and she's not hurting you. You're doing every-thing just right."

I twist my neck until I can look over my shoulder at her. She's kneeling behind me, smiling her big smile. Her flinty eyes are warm: rain-washed slate.

"I am?" I ask.

"You are. You're doing very well. Would you like to help Allyn take care of the bunnies and Harry a few days a week?"

"I, uh, I have a job." Does she think I don't work? Fur-people need to pay rent, too. "But I could come in the evenings."

"That would be lovely," Mistress says. "I'd very much like to treat you to dinner on the nights you're here."

She would? She took me down to the club's buffet after our short scene, which was so kind of her, but I didn't think she'd want to eat with me again. Mice don't make the best dinner companions.

"Try running your fingertip, very gently, along the bunny's tummy," Mistress suggests.

Barely ruffling the tips of Cupcake's fur, I stroke as instructed.

Cupcake stretches out her back legs and wedges her head further under my calf.

"Very good, Georgie," Mistress praises me. She reaches over my shoulder, takes a bunny brush from Lacey, and hands it to me. "Try brushing her back first so you don't startle her."

I run the brush down Cupcake's back, as much as I can reach with the bunny pressed against my leg. When she doesn't flinch or try to get away, I brush her back until her fur is flat and smooth, then very tentatively touch her belly with it.

She flicks her back feet, but then relaxes.

I brush her tummy until it's as smooth as her back.

Lacey, who has been moving around the loose circle of Littles, squats in front of me. "Georgie, you're a natural. Cupcake's coat looks amazing and she's so relaxed with you."

"Thank you. It's not so different from the way I brush my fursuit."

"I can see you do an excellent job with that," Lacey says, tipping her head from side to side admiringly. "My buns are in good hands."

"So are Maude's," Chess says, crossing his arms over his broad chest and grinning.

I twist my neck and look over my shoulder at Mistress. Surely, she'll be angry—?

No, I should know better. She's unflappable. Even better, she's smiling her big smile, even as she shakes her head at the Chairman.

Mistress has a sense of humor, too.

[The End]

TWELVE

an inglorious tail

MASTER TEN AND FLEUR – TEN

OPERATION: *Glory Hole*

Location: Blunts

Time: 20:08

The shadows are busy tonight.

They began scrabbling two days ago after Javier interfered with my usual rota. Some bullshit about Fleur needing a break after drama with her boyfriend.

Nigel, I think his name is.

I should have hunted Nigel down and made him an X months ago when she hurt her ankle. I know she didn't fall. She's a dancer. I've seen her balance on one foot, in stilettos, for a half-hour. Outside of the martial artists I know, Fleur's got the lowest center of gravity I've seen. She doesn't fall. She didn't fall.

She was pushed.

I'd have dealt with the abusive asshole if she hadn't lied to me about how she got hurt.

Liars don't deserve my protection.

Fleur's desperate for attention; she can barely set limits on her submission. She needs someone to protect her despite her lies.

The shadows are loud tonight.

I stuff that one down into the darkness. I'm no one's hero.

I check my watch, even though I'm hyper-aware that there's still nearly an hour to go until our rescheduled scene.

Fifty-two minutes until sinking into a scene drives away the shadows.

I contemplate calling Fleur and see if she can be ready early.

Discard that thought as a demi-shadow.

I don't do well with changes to my routine. It's in place to keep the shadows at bay. Even though a scene will help banish them, starting it earlier than scheduled may send me into the scene in the wrong head-space.

She may be a liar, but she deserves better than that from me.

"Do you have somewhere to be?"

I look up from my watch into Javier's smiling face. He pulls an armchair over to mine—set on my own where I can look out of the smoking lounge's panoramic windows at the City's lights—and offers me one of his disgusting cigarettes.

I shake my head and show him my unlit cigar.

Sometimes curling my trigger finger around something helps stave off the shadows.

Javier lights up with a wooden match before offering the match to me.

With a nod of thanks, I light my cigar and take a few puffs to get the cherry established. It's a Padron Family Reserve 50, rich and earthy. I don't want to think about how much of my monthly dues are going towards the little coil of aged leaves between my fingers. Better to just enjoy it and not consider the cost too closely.

"No," I answer his question, which is still hanging in the air like the smoke from our respective cancer sticks. "Just keeping an eye on the time."

"Was your scene with Fleur rescheduled to tonight?"

I nod after taking another warm puff that paints my palate with the flavor of coffee.

"Could I encourage you to put it off another day or two? Our lovely flower needs some time."

"No," I say tersely. She may need some time but I can't wait anymore.

"Briar's available tonight," Javier offers.

I know she is. I can read the sub roster as well as anyone else. I don't need Briar's brand of bitchy resistance. I need DirtyGurl's sardonic, shadow-banishing submission . . . Fleur is an acceptable substitute.

"No," I repeat.

Javier sighs and puffs.

"I've been meaning to catch up with you," Javier says. "I sense you're out of sorts with the recent changes."

"You mean Logan's bullshit?"

"And Brenna's new master's application to join us."

I shift in my chair before I can still myself. I take a deep pull on the cigar to smoke out the rush of shadows that accompanies thinking about *him*.

"Logan takes off for the better part of a year," I say. "Then he strolls back in here and tells us how to treat the subs he's ignored for months, like we don't know how to take care of our own. And everyone treats him like the second coming." I shrug. "Feels wrong."

"The house submissives are not in a good state, mon gars. Surely you can see that."

"I see Briar bein' Briar. I see Pence bein' Pence. What else am I supposed to see?"

Javier crosses one leg over the other. "I'm going to say this not because I'm criticizing but because of my respect for you. You, of all of us, were closest to DirtyGurl. She was miserable. She was pulling further and further away, further into her own head. Nothing any of us did stopped that downward spiral—"

"She's a fucking adult and responsible for her own headspace. If she was miserable, she should have *said* something to someone. We're not their fucking therapists, J."

"No, we're not," Javier agrees. "But as dominants who care about them, we must be sensitive to their mental health."

Sensitive. Everyone has to be so *sensitive* now. I don't come to Blunts to be sensitive. I come to beat back the shadows by beating some asses. What the fuck am I getting out of this if I have to be *sensitive* to the people who are supposed to be here because they want to submit to me?

"Thought they all saw that therapist. What's her name?"

"Lydia," Javier answers. "They have an entirely voluntary group session with her every other week."

"Good, that should take care of them."

"Ten," Javier says, his voice full of reproach. "It's not enough. Intense scenes break down a submissive's mental and emotional defenses. You are *known* for intense scenes."

I scoff at him. "So're you."

"Yes, but the submissive I've been with for nearly five years didn't just resign from the club."

So that's what this is really about. DirtyGurl walking shook Javier's faith in me. Well, I don't need his fucking approval.

I lean forward and get in his face. "You can't keep a submissive for longer than a year. You just don't collar house subs, so it's not a club issue and none of us stick our noses in your business. Don't lecture me, J. Things get stale. The male of the species isn't built for monogamy. We've talked this around before. DirtyGurl and I were stale. That's all there was to it. We'd run our course and needed to move on. We lasted a lot longer than you and your revolving door of ice princesses. So keep your opinions to your fucking self."

Javier stares back, not flinching. "Your actions toward her outside of Chess's office say otherwise."

I shake my head. "Like you haven't ordered a sub to her knees."

"You weren't in scene. She used her safe word."

"You said it, we weren't in scene."

"A submissive's safe word must *always* be respected. No matter where or when."

"Gotta agree to disagree," I say, sitting back and puffing on my cigar, blowing out a cloud of blue smoke that obscures the City's twinkling lights. "Whole point of a safe word is to stop a scene."

"You took off your belt and threatened to hit her with it, Ten. That's either a scene or it's assault and battery. You tell me which."

The shadows crowd closer. Scrabble harder. I can hear them over my own breathing, the regular thud of my heart.

"She tell you that?" If she did, I bet *he* pushed her into it. My DirtyGurl's not a snitch.

"She didn't say a word. I've seen the CCTV recording."

Wonder who showed that to him? It wouldn't be our resident security expert and house submissive whisperer, would it? Fucking Logan. Everything comes back to fucking Logan.

"I've hit her with that belt a thousand times. She knows I'd never injure her with it. She wasn't afraid of me. She sassed back at me like she always does. Fucking mouthiest submissive I've ever met. No idea why I wasted so much time on her."

Javier tips his head back and blows a long stream of smoke toward the curved glass above us. "If that's what you truly think, I am extremely sorry for you."

"I don't need your fucking pity any more than I need your judgment." I check my watch. It's still early but I can legitimately walk away from this conversation and get the dungeon ready. I stab out my cigar. "Last time we talk about this."

Javier blinks up at the glass ceiling. "Be gentle with our flower. Tell her if she has no other plans, I'd like her to come home with me tonight."

"She has other plans," I growl.

Javier tips his head forward and levels a hard stare at me. "Don't hurt our trésor to assuage your bruised ego, mon vieux. DirtyGurl never wanted my protection. Fleur is a different matter."

"You're collaring her?"

"She doesn't want my collar. And you have no business offering her yours in the state-of-mind you're in. Not for a scene and certainly not for a night. Don't take her home with you."

The shadows gibber and draw in tight enough I feel their breath on my neck.

"That a threat?"

"I am not so stupid as to threaten you. It's a statement. For the sake of a submissive we both care about, do not take her home with you tonight. Let me take care of her."

"You think I can't take care of my submissive?"

"I don't think you can take care of Fleur tonight. That is all I'm saying or will say. Do the right thing, Ten." He tips his head back to the ceiling.

"Night," I tell him before I turn on my heel and stride through the lounge, tossing my butt into the trash can by the bar. With Javier yapping and the shadows scrabbling, I couldn't even enjoy it like I should have. Fucking waste.

The eyes I'm looking into—pale when I want them to be brown—widen as I point to the partition I've pulled into the middle of the medical suite.

"Use a pillow if you need it," I tell her, before I walk around the screen.

The partition is twelve by eight. It completely blocks off the side of the room she's on. I can't see her and she can't see me except as shadows on the screen's white fabric. I pull out one of my knives and poke a hole in the screen. Twisting the knife, I widen the hole until it's just big enough for my dick.

Tucking the knife away, I unbutton my leathers, take myself in hand and tap the head against the screen until I've got a semi, then thrust it through the hole.

"Suck me, bitch."

She wouldn't dare disobey. Fleur's not a sweet sub; her submission can be cold and grudging. It's just that you never hit bottom with her. Even with DirtyGurl, I eventually mapped her boundaries. That kernel of self that just won't yield.

Fleur's kernel is missing.

Despite my command and the knowledge that she'll obey, the hot, slick lick of her tongue over my tip comes as a shock. I couldn't see her move; I couldn't anticipate her touch. It ripples through me and tightens my balls.

"More."

I hear her shift.

Pillow-soft wetness envelops my head. The firm tip of her tongue prods at my slit. With the screen between us, without her looking at me for direction and dominance, I'm free to close my eyes and just feel.

"Lollypop it," I growl.

With a dizzying twirl around my sensitive ridge, wet heat laps around my head. My thighs tighten. My abs. My balls. The slick underside of her tongue flicks again and again against my tip. I reach up and grip the edge of the screen.

"Suck my head into your mouth."

Achingly slowly, she widens her lips and pulls me into the furnace of her mouth. I stifle a groan.

"Back off and blow."

Cool air replaces heat; I shiver with pleasure.

"Take me all the way down."

She's not warmed up. It will be a struggle for her, despite the many hours she's served here on her knees.

She sucks me into her hot mouth again, licks, and tries to swallow me down. I'm too big for her to take in the first gulp. Her tongue spasms as my tip hits her tonsils, triggering what little gag reflex she has left. The soft tissues at the back of her throat press in all around my corona. I lean in, pushing that half-inch deeper. She chokes and swallows.

"Fuck, good," I groan. "More, little bitch."

I don't give her more than a second's mercy, shifting my hips back so she gets a sip of air, before I squeeze my ass-muscles and shove forward. She swallows desperately, her throat pulsing, tongue fluttering. If I could see through the screen, her delicate-boned face would be turned up to me, streaming eyes pleading, cheeks hollowed, the cords of her throat straining under her skin. The mental image does as much for me as the sensations.

I give her another sip of air before I fuck her face. She's well-trained. She holds position while I shove in and pull back, cursing as my pleasure mounts. She coughs when I let her breathe but doesn't whimper in protest at my rough use.

"That's right. You know what you deserve, slut."

Fleur hums and swallows.

"Impale yourself on that thick cock. Show me how much you want it."

She gulps and presses forward, her nose nudging my lower belly through the screen. The screen grows wet against my thighs as I thrust faster, muscles tightening, balls lifting. I growl as the tension builds and that draws the first whimper out of her. I know her whimpers. That's discomfort, not true pain.

"Take it, little bitch. Open your fucking mouth and swallow when I come."

She chokes and coughs against my hammering. Her noises beat back the shadows, opening the way for a release that clears my body and mind. I yank on the edge of the screen as I go up on my toes, every muscle snapping taut. My back bows, smashing my groin into Fleur's face as I come, spurting down her throat.

She swallows and coughs, swallows, and sputters. I steady myself with a groan and press my forehead against the screen while I catch my breath.

"Lick me clean and sit back."

It takes her a moment to recover, then her tongue begins to

move. My eyes cross when she sucks my softening, oversensitive cock. She releases me, damp but no longer messy. I pull back through the ripped, ruined screen and tuck myself away.

"Compose yourself then come kneel," I tell her.

"Yes, Master Ten." Her voice is raspier than a two-pack-a-day smoker, which makes me smile as I find some wet wipes.

She walks around the screen, putting one foot in front of the other, that model-walk that she and some of the other dancers do so well. Sure, she fell.

She sinks to her knees in front of me and immediately settles into the perfect position. There's no bitchy defiance. Fleur's submission may be grudging, but once she's in the headspace, she's perfect.

A Dom could just keep spiraling down and down into her.

I wipe her face. She knows I like to see streaked mascara after a scene, and that's all she's wearing. I make sure to get off every smear, so there's nothing but her alabaster skin under my fingers. I stroke her cheeks and temples long after her face is clean, giving her the aftercare she's earned. Her eyelids get heavy as I caress her. I could take her home with me. Take my time fucking her, maybe even give her an orgasm or two, now that the shadows aren't threatening. Fleur's come home with me before; she knows what to expect.

But Javier's words are scrabbling around at the edges of my thoughts now, instead of the shadows.

So I say, "I bumped into Javier before the scene. He said if you don't have plans tonight, he'd like you to go home with him."

She smiles. A soft, sweet smile that still carries the echoes of subspace. At least I gave her that tonight.

"I'll go find him," she says mistily.

I clear my throat. "You know if you're having trouble, Fleur, you only have to call me."

The haze retreats from her gaze. "Thank you, Master Ten."

I give her a few beats to say more. When she doesn't, I lean down and kiss her forehead. "Have a good night. You have my permission to come if you want to masturbate. Tell Javier he's an asshole."

She giggles. "I'd never disobey you, sir, but I may edit that message before I deliver it, for the sake of my hide."

I run my hand over her soft, midnight hair. Wrong color. I push my thoughts on. "You here over the weekend?"

She nods. "Both days."

"Keep a night open for me. I want your ass."

She wrinkles her nose. She says she hates anal; she'll offer almost anything before she gives me her ass. But, just like that face-fucking, her body says otherwise. "Yes, sir."

I offer her my hand and when she takes it, help her to her feet. "Plan to come home with me on Saturday."

"Yes, sir. Cappa's staying with me right now. I don't like leaving him alone, after, well, you know."

I know. It's not my problem, since it happened outside the club, but I know about it and I'm willing to include him if he's struggling, even though I rarely play with Cappa. "Tell him to come, too."

Her smile's wide and bright, happily anticipating a threesome, as she slips out of the door of the medical suite. "Goodnight, sir."

A shadow stretches away from the door, toward my feet, as she closes it behind her.

[The End]

THIRTEEN

a vexatious tail

CHAIRMAN CHESS, MASTER EMMETT, GUEST, AND TESSA – TESSA

I TAKE a moment to smooth my hair before I walk into the sauna.

I've been waxed, plucked, moisturized, trimmed, deep-conditioned, and massaged. A treat from the club for my birthday last week. My Master told me to meet him in the sauna for a birthday treat from him. I'm a few minutes early, but I want to be positioned perfectly, my newly burnished hide gleaming with sweat, when he arrives. Watching me pose brings my Master so much happiness.

He's been without for so long; he deserves every drop.

I open the sauna and walk in.

Two naked men lying on the benches lift their heads and look at me.

"My apologies," I say. "I thought this was empty."

There's a little sign on the outside of the sauna that members and house submissives are supposed to flip over when the sauna is occupied. I checked before I opened the door. Maybe they forgot to turn it over.

"Come in, Tessa," says one of the men, sitting up.

It's Master Emmett. Even without the Harry Potter-ish glasses he usually wears, I recognize his mop of brown hair. He's a newer member. I've never done a scene with him. He usually does the "group" scenes with Master Al and his submissive, Mackie. I'm not sure I've ever been alone in a room with him before.

But he's still a master of Blunts. I bow my head to him and walk into the middle of the sauna, closing the door behind me. I take a deep breath of the cedar-scented, humid air, center my feet on the hot, wooden planks, and tuck my hands behind me in the resting inspection position all Blunts house submissives are taught.

"How may I serve you, Master Emmett?" I ask.

The other man, blond and hairy-chested, sits up and drapes his hand over one knee. He has an erection, which my eyes skitter away from. I'm not sure why. I've seen a lot of erections since coming to work at Blunts.

"They really do act like slaves," the blond man says. I don't recognize him. He's not a member, so he must be Master Emmett's guest. "When you told me, I didn't believe it."

I swallow, trying not to be weirded out by him talking about me like I'm not here. Sometimes guests don't understand the lifestyle. Members are supposed to explain, but maybe Master Emmett didn't think it was important since they're only in the spa, not upstairs in the dungeons.

Master Emmett doesn't say anything to his guest, or to me.

Instead, he twirls his finger in the air. I take that as a signal to turn around.

I don't want to. It's more than the way I sometimes resist in scenes to make my Dom exert his mastery. Something about this has the small hairs on the back of my neck prickling with more than the damp heat. I'm glad I'm wearing a bathing suit. I'm used to being naked with the members, but in the spa we're supposed to wear bathing suits and I have, figuring my Master will take it off me when he's ready.

Even with the bathing suit, I don't want to turn my back on these two men.

Master Emmett frowns and twirls his finger again.

I take a breath in. Let it out slowly. He's a member; I'm a house submissive. We haven't arranged a scene, but he's not asking me to do anything out of the ordinary. It's barely even submission.

Still, my gut balks.

"Doesn't she know that signal?" the blond man asks.

Of course I know that signal. I'm not an idiot.

"Tessa." It's not quite a command, but it's only a semitone away.

I swallow, lift my chin, and turn slowly.

While my back's to them, the blond man says, "Make her bend over. Show me that fucking ass. She is *ripe*."

I stare at the sauna's closed door, swallowing hard. I haven't negotiated for any of this. Objectification and degradation aren't hard limits for me when they're part of scenes. This doesn't feel like a scene. It feels real.

It feels hateful.

"No," I say to the door.

There's movement behind me.

A hand sinks into my hair. The hair I've had trimmed and deep-conditioned and brushed until it's a perfect, straight fall to my shoulders so that my Master would see it and stroke it and tell me how beautiful his puppy is.

Emmett grabs a handful of hair at the nape of my neck, too far away from my scalp. I blink at the pinch. That's not the way Doms are taught to grab hair.

His hand pushes my head forward until my forehead smacks the hot wood of the door.

"Did you say *no* to my guest, Tessa?" Master Emmett hisses close to my ear.

"Yes, sir," I respond, hearing the tremor in my voice, feeling the shaking spreading through me. Everything about this is so wrong. "We haven't scheduled a scene. I don't know who your guest is and I don't agree to scene with him. Please let me go. I'm going to be late to meet Master Chess."

The cruel grip on my hair relaxes. Emmett smooths my hair and steps back.

"Of course. I wouldn't want to make you late." His hand drops to the edge of my bikini bottom. He finds a welt from where my Master belted me yesterday and pinches it hard enough to make me wince. "Wouldn't want to earn you a punishment."

I open my mouth to retort when the sauna door opens in a swirl of steam. Chess's dark eyes move over my face and the smile drains out of them.

"Tessa, darling?"

"Sir, this one's already occupied. Master Emmett must have forgotten to flip the sign over. We should use another."

Chess's eyes track over my shoulder then return to my face. "Is that so?"

"Yes, sir."

I hear Master Emmett move behind me. "Oh, don't go. If you were planning a scene in here, we'd be delighted to watch. Chess, this is my guest, Hans."

Chess's eyes stay on my face as he nods to the blond man. "Hans, it's a pleasure to meet you. I'm afraid I don't share Tessa, so I'll have to decline your offer, Emmett. Enjoy the sauna. Be careful not to stay in too long. All the heat, it can cloud your judgment."

Emmett and Hans laugh.

Chess holds his hand out to me. I slip my fingers into his and let him lead me away.

He takes me into one of the spa offices instead of another sauna room. He lays a folded towel on the floor and gestures to it as he pulls up a chair. I fold down onto my knees, put my hands behind me, and bow my head.

His warm hand settles on my crown. "Take three deep breaths. Let them out slowly. Count of five. Then you'll tell me what happened that's upset you."

I follow his instruction letter for letter. All the weirdness of how I felt in the sauna drains away under my Master's warm hand, his firm direction. Did I misread the situation? Did I overreact?

"Bring your paws in front of you and hold them in begging position one," Chess says after I release my third, slow breath.

I do. My hands are steady as I cross them in front of me at the height of my breasts.

"That's very good, my sweet puppy," my Master says, his voice rich with praise. He guides my hands gently down to my lap. "Now, tell me what happened."

"I think-I think I overreacted, sir."

"Overreacted to what?"

"No-nothing. Nothing really happened. I just-it felt wrong."

"I see. Don't think about it. Tell me what happened moment by moment."

"I walked into the sauna. Master Emmett and his guest were already in there but they hadn't turned the sign over. Master Emmett told me to come in. He wanted me to display myself for his guest. I didn't-I didn't want to, sir. I resisted."

"Why didn't you want to, darling?"

"I don't know, sir. Everything just felt wrong. Master Emmett's guest, that Hans guy, he kept talking about me like I wasn't there."

"Did you feel afraid?" Chess asks, his voice dropping.

"I know I shouldn't have, sir. I could have said my safe word or walked out—"

"Darling, listen to my question. Did you feel afraid?"

"Yes, sir."

He draws me forward until I can rest my cheek on his knee. His leg hairs tickle my cheek. He's wearing a bathing suit; it's as casually as I've ever seen him dress. We should be relaxing together in the steamy heat and instead he's comforting me because I overreacted to a Dom I don't know well and a stranger.

"Sir, I'm sorry. I think it just threw me that they were in there when I wasn't expecting them to be. It's been a lovely day. I don't want to ruin it. Can we please go back to the sauna?"

"I think I'd rather stay out of the sauna right now so I'm not tempted to strangle Emmett and his guest."

That makes me smile against his knee. "That would tarnish your image, sir."

"Yes, it would. Do you know what else tarnishes my image, my sweet puppy?" He doesn't wait for me to answer. "Submissives who are afraid to be alone with the members of my club."

"I'm sorry, sir."

"You have nothing to be sorry for. I will have a talk with Emmett both about setting scene boundaries and ensuring his guests behave appropriately. And I think it's time everyone knows you're not available for scenes."

I'm not? Chess asked me several days ago how I felt about being exclusive with him and I said I'd like to, but I thought it was something for the future. Possibly the distant future. I lift my head and look into his dark eyes.

There's a smile back in them, behind the flicker of protective anger. "Yes, my darling," he says. "That means what you think it means."

I put my head back down on his knee and break position to hug his shin, closing my eyes as happiness floods me. Master Emmett's cruelty, his guest's nastiness, the lost scene, they all fade away to nothing. My Master wants us to be exclusive. He wants everyone to know I'm *his*.

I doubt this is the birthday treat my Master had in mind when he told me to meet him in the sauna, but it's the best birthday treat I can imagine.

[The members and house submissives of Blunts will return in Daddy P.I. 3.0]

THE
DADDY P.I.
CASEFILES
BOOK 3
DADDY P.I.
3.0
E. J. FROST

about the author

Reader, bunny-wrangler, fire-spinner, and writer of things. I like my science hard and my romance harder.

Constitutionally incapable of settling into a genre, I bounce in and out of contemporary mystery, space opera, and paranormal romance, all with a decidedly kinky twist.

Sign up to my newsletter for a free book, sneak peeks, and updates:

https://dl.bookfunnel.com/r94ra9ilza

Need more Blunts Tales? Get early access and exclusive stories in my Patreon: https://www.patreon.com/ejfrost

Bring cake.

If you've enjoyed *Blunts Tales 2*, please consider leaving a review on your platform of choice. Reviews mean everything to independent authors!

facebook.com/emmafrostuk

twitter.com/ejfrostuk

instagram.com/emmafrostuk

bookbub.com/authors/e-j-frost

goodreads.com/ejfrost

tiktok.com/@ejfrostauthor

patreon.com/ejfrost

Snowburn

M/F , Scifi Romance.

Unleash the monster. Save the girl.

Hale Hauser is a Company killer. Perfectly engineered, highly trained, superbly effective. But when ordered to assassinate his own kind, Hale rebels, and the Company buries him in a hole so deep that no one has ever escaped.

After escaping, Hale hides on Kuseros, a backwater Colony on the Deep Frontier. He begins a new life as Sandringham Snow, pilot and smuggler. Hired by Kez, a local runner, to retrieve a box of black-market glands, Hale follows her through the maze of strange loyalties and twisted customs of Kuseros' underground gangs. In payment, he takes the one thing only a woman can give him, and discovers the one thing his new life is missing.

But Kez has a secret, which will threaten them both. To protect her, Hale must unleash the monster. Can he control the killer inside long enough to discover the truth before it destroys them? Or will he lose everything just as he's found it?

Read *Snowburn* here, free to read with a Kindle Unlimited subscription: **https://books2read.com/u/m2Z9ko**.

www.ingramcontent.com/pod-product-compliance
Lightning Source LLC
Chambersburg PA
CBHW071435130726
47997CB00006B/2093